I0557592

Summer Ice

My Life at the Bidwell

Diana K. Perkins

Copyright © 2015 by Diana K. Perkins
1st Edition – August 1, 2015
ISBN
978-0-9891994-1-4 (Paperback)
978-0-9891994-3-8 (eBook)
All rights reserved.

No part of this book may be reproduced or transmitted in any form or by any means, electronic or mechanical, including photocopying, recording or by any information storage and retrieval system, without permission in writing from the author.

Disclaimer: This is a fictional novel. Any resemblance to actual lives or persons is purely accidental and should not be taken as fact, although to bring realism to the novel's setting in Coventry, Connecticut, some of the characters, buildings, businesses, churches and roads referred to are or were actual people, structures or institutions.

Author's Notes: This novel is set in the decades between the 1870s and the 1900s, a time of great transformation in the world. Some of the historical references are to actual events; see historic convergences and divergences at the end of the book.

Produced by:
Shetucket Hollow Press
1 Shetucket Drive, Windham, CT 06280-1530

Author's website: http://www.dianakperkins.com

Acknowledgements

I want to thank the people of Coventry who gave of their time to share life stories and information. Without your help I could not have written this book. I especially want to thank William Jobbagy, whose thorough history of Coventry was a wonderful source of information. Also, a posthumous thank you to Arnold Carlson, who shared interesting insights into Coventry's past. Thank you to the Bidwell Tavern, where history drips from the rafters and which offers inspirational wings.

I want to thank my readers Faith Kenton, Christine Pattee, Terry Cote and Michelle Giffin, whose thoughtful feedback made this a much better story. I also want to sincerely thank my faithful editor, Blanche Boucher, who never fails to correct my grammar and improve my work.

The Bidwell House, looking east, early 1900s.
Note the sidewalk on the south side of Main Street (right) and
the stream just beyond. The north side has newly-laid tracks for
the trolley.

The Bidwell House, looking northwest, late 1800s.

Dedicated to

My friends in Coventry, Connecticut

Diana K. Perkins

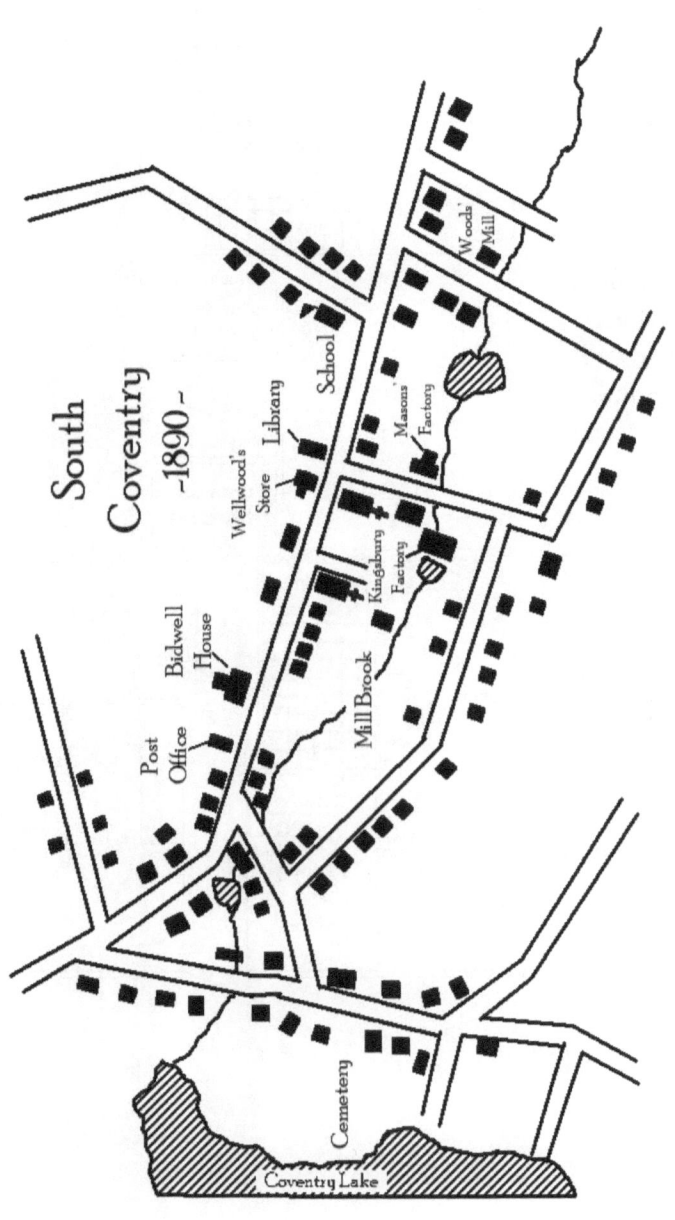

South
Coventry
~1890~

Post
Office

Bidwell
House

Wellwood's
Store

Library

School

Woods'
Mill

Masons'
Factory

Kingsbury
Factory

Mill Brook

Cemetery

Coventry Lake

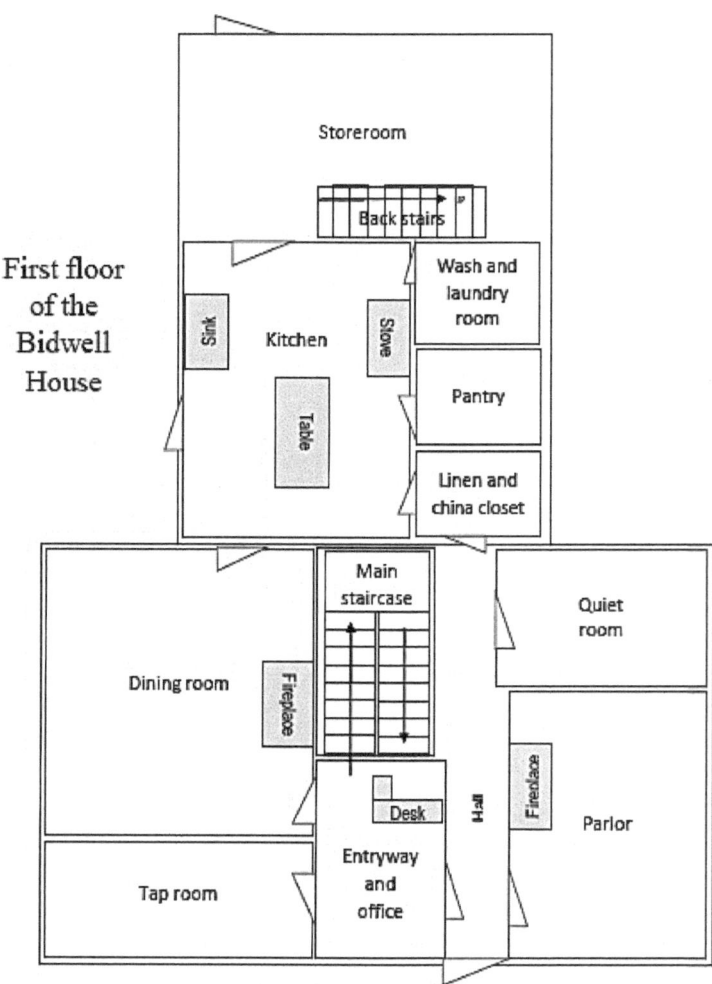

First floor
of the
Bidwell
House

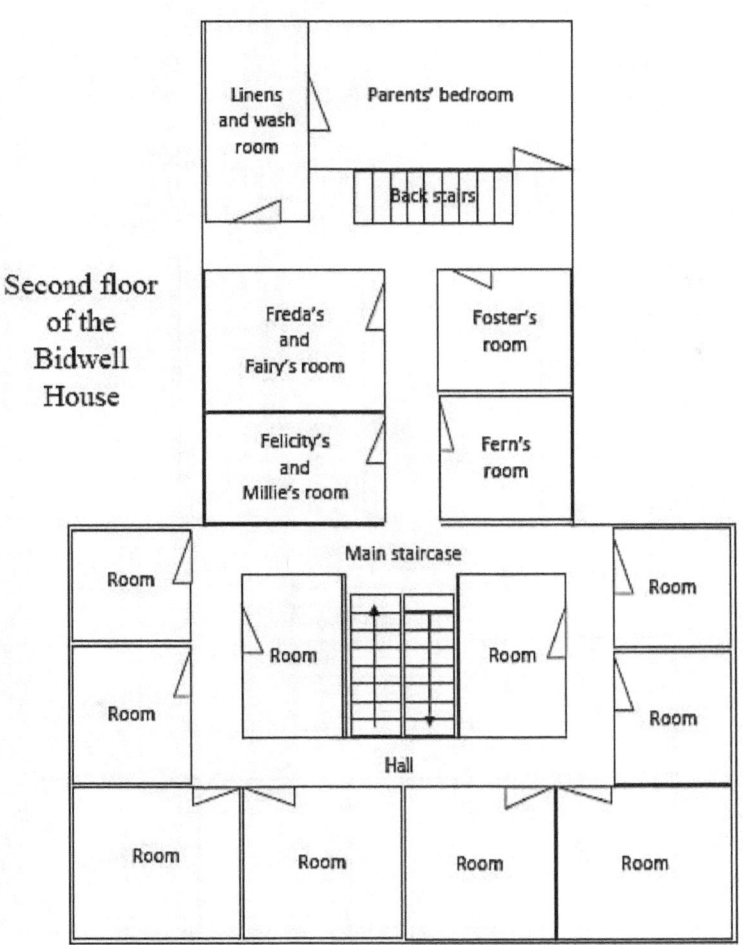

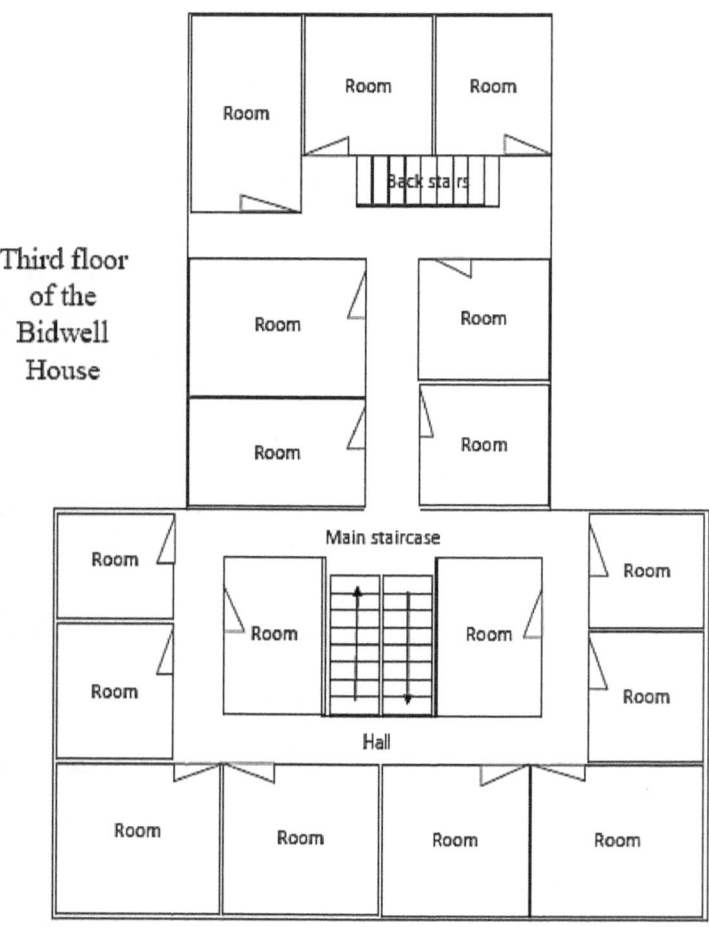

Third floor
of the
Bidwell
House

Every town has its royalty: its wealthy, its old established families, its people of renown. My town was no different. But my town, like other towns, also had its share of deadbeats, illiterates, drunkards and poor. Towns are born, grow, decline; they inhale and exhale, and if enough of its citizens care, they are vibrant rich communities. When I was growing up my town was still in its glorious youth.

-   Millicent Submit White

Diana K. Perkins

Part 1

Diana K. Perkins

Chapter 1

What was it that endowed me with the fortitude to survive not only near physical starvation but also starvation of the spirit? It could not have been my blood ties; I knew of none. It could not have been my family, which seemed as fickle as a young girl's dreams. It could only have been an impossible ember that smoldered within, waiting to flare into flame when the yearning breath of possibility blew upon it.

Strangely I remember what I think of as my first bath. I was in the kitchen sink with my twin, Felicity. The late afternoon sunlight's almost horizontal rays blazed through the window over the sink, its warm yellow glow highlighting my mother and us and seeming to throw the rest of the room into darkness.

Mother—I will call her my mother—finished bathing me first, using the pan of warm water on the side of the sink to rinse me, pat me dry and wrap me. I was more robust than Felicity and Mother would take me out of the bath to give Felicity more attention.

My father watched from the kitchen table, having already settled down to a cup of tea and the newspaper spread out in the lamp's golden circle of light. He leaned into the table as the evening light faded and reached out to turn up the lamp wick. Shuffling the pages, he held them open with one hand and took a sip of tea with the other. My mother unwrapped the towel, slipped me into my flannel nightgown, lowered me to the floor to crawl about, and turned back to

Felicity. Nipper, the fat cocker, wiggled over to me and licked my freshly washed face as I tried to push her away.

For some reason that evening is etched into my mind: the sink under the window full of warm sudsy water, my father's face lit from above as he bent over the paper, the dog sidling over to me. Of such things are lives made, snippets of memories pressed into the pages of our minds, all bound together into the ledger of our worldly existence, and all put on the shelf or scattered to the wind or thrown into the fire once it is all done.

Mine is a ledger that is yellowed and well-used, with some sections crossed out or written over, those times I don't wish to remember or times when I learned an important lesson. Hindsight—always hindsight—gave me the glass in which I could best reflect upon the past and project into the future. So here I look back through that glass and share the tale of my sometimes difficult, sometimes joyful youth.

Chapter 2

My family owned an inn where we gave weary travelers a comfortable place to rest at the end of their day. It was on a main thoroughfare in South Coventry, Connecticut, and even though our family was the Whites, the inn was called the Bidwell House, Solomon Bidwell having built it in 1822 and run it with his son Lyman into the 1850s. My father, Fitzgerald White, came into some money on the death of my grandfather and purchased the inn two decades ago, in 1874. I was born two years later. He continued to work at the box factory to help with the inn's mortgage and upkeep during thinner times. Although he was a good breadwinner he was not as handy at the fixings and finishings of the inn's many needs.

The inn was a large four-story affair, broad across the front where it faced Main Street, with an ell in the back. Cut into the hill were several steps that led our guests to the street and the sidewalk that followed Main Street and Mill Brook beyond. Several large maples surrounding our inn gave us comfortable shade in the summer. The inn had thirty-three rooms, five of which housed our family. The kitchen was on the first floor in the back at the corner of the ell and ran almost to the end. The family lived above the kitchen, with a back staircase giving us easy access to cooking and laundering facilities to meet the needs of our guests and maintain their rooms. In the front entryway the main desk had a fine wire running from the door to a bell at the back stairs where we could hear it ring from our bedrooms or from the kitchen, thereby alerting us to anyone entering or leaving. A large barn in back of the inn, not far from the ell, accommodated our guests' horses and coaches. In the inn's front section the room that had once been the post office we now used as a taproom for guests who wanted to enjoy a cigar and beer after supper. Into the hill behind the inn a large root cellar had been dug, where we stored ice cut from the lake and covered in sawdust; it would last for months and keep food from spoiling. A henhouse conveniently close by gave us eggs and chickens. The village was full of mills, a good general store, a library and several shops, most within walking distance. A large and lovely lake crowned the top of the hill that our Main Street climbed.

The village of Coventry was midway between Willimantic and Manchester, both bustling mill towns. The lake fed a brook that had steep drops, providing enough water power for sixteen mills spanning the distance from Coventry Lake (sometimes called by its Indian name, Wangumbaug) to where the brook met the Willimantic River. Over the years the mill buildings had changed hands and purposes a number of times. When I was young in the 1870s there was a grist mill, a spoke and carriage wheel shop, a blacksmith's, a cider and vinegar mill, a saw mill, a paper mill and a shingle mill. Several textile mills—for silk, cotton, satinette and shoddy—also utilized the stream's power. But to me the most important mills were the Kingsbury Box Factory, where my father worked, which made paper and cardboard boxes, and the Mason Cartridge factory, which made bullets; I was told it had supplied a great number of them for the Union Army in the Civil War. The cartridge factory was where my boyfriend worked, when I grew old enough to have a boyfriend.

The village was bustling and had all the stores and services we needed. The Wellwood general store was a few doors down the street and the library where my sister spent so much time was nearly next door to that. Two churches were almost across the street from the inn, and not very far away were our schoolhouse and a grange. The post office and town building were close by. A barbershop and social club were handy for the men. A railroad depot with a coach that ran through town served us well. Outlying farms provided fresh vegetables, fruits and meat to our lively little community. Years later a trolley track was laid all the way from Willimantic, and on weekends it usually brought us city laborers seeking to escape from the sweltering tenements and relax by the lake.

Chapter 3

My father, Fitzy as his friends called him, was a gregarious fellow, the center of attention in most gatherings. His commanding presence, easygoing demeanor and willingness to chatter about all manner of daily life drew people to him. I rarely remember him quiet except when he was reading his paper, which he was very particular about. No one should open or read the paper before he did; he would notice a crease out of alignment and let out a bellow. But such times of irritation were rare with him. A large and cheerful countenance projected from nearly every atom of his being. His great red moustache flared out beyond his full cheeks, sharp but not too sharp. On occasional mornings he would let my sister Felicity and me watch him as he groomed and dressed that lovely moustache.

Fitzy was well suited for his manager's position at the box factory. The workers under him respected him and found him fair and easy to work for. If a job was not being done well he would talk to the worker in a manner that almost always brought improvement afterward. Some of the other managers may have envied his way with the workers, but if they did they never spoke of it.

He had a gusto for life, a hearty appetite, and the ability to down a large quantity of beer without a noticeable change in his demeanor. He enjoyed a laugh with his chums and watched the ladies with them, but he was devoted to our mother and vowed he would never stray.

Though not a particularly religious man he told us the basic value we should live by was the Golden Rule and if we followed that we would all do fine in life. His lack of interest in organized religion while owning an inn so near two churches caused the pastors to endeavor to work their charms on him. Each in turn would come to supper, always resulting in an evening of laughter and lively conversation.

Our mother Florence White was, as my father frequently exclaimed, "sweet as a ripe peach." She was in most ways the opposite of her husband, introspective, demure, and industrious. While Fitzy was a good man, amiable and well-liked, he was not the hardest-working member of the family. Florence was the worker, the organizer, the real backbone of the family, and although it wasn't obvious, tough as nails. She was his physical opposite too, slight and delicate, with clear skin and silky golden hair she wore in a bun that wouldn't interfere with her daily chores.

Father would often come home and exclaim, "You're working too hard, Flo. Why don't you take a break?" To which my mother would gently snort out of her nose, "Humph. And who do you think will do all the work?" while she continued folding the towels she'd just brought in from the line. As he leaned to give her a warm kiss on the cheek she would elbow him away, bent on finishing her task.

Of course we all helped her. That is what a large family does. She was fortunate to have us five girls and a boy, all with similar coloring, not as fair as Mother nor as ruddy as Father but with thick rich manes of auburn hair and eyes that were almost green. All of them except me–I had dark hair and dark eyes.

The oldest of us White girls was named Freda. I sometimes think that Father wanted a boy and when he couldn't call her Fred he called her Freda, pronouncing it with a short "e". Freda was tall and robust, outgoing and much like Father except she was a bit of a bully. She knew her place in the family. As the firstborn she could boss the younger kids and push them around.

The second child, almost two years younger, was Fern. Fern was as different from Father as Freda was like him. Surprisingly Fern wasn't like Mother either. Tall and wiry, she could withstand the pinches and pushes of her older sister. She was bookish and could often be found scrunched into a sunlit corner or hunched over a table with her face pushed into well-worn pages. Fern was fortunate that the inn was not far from the library. She could run there after school or when she had free time, pick out a book and run home. And run home Fern must, for as Mother worked hard to keep the inn going, Freda felt responsible for making sure the rest of the children helped, even if she herself did little of it.

Fairy came next, and sadly for the rest of us she was not at all blithe and light like a fairy but more like Freda and Father, a big rough girl. She would often collude with Freda to bully us other kids into doing her work.

I came next, but that is another story.

Around the time I joined the family, Felicity White was born. She was the most precious girl and just like Mother. She was pretty and gentle and sweet, kind and bright. Her only flaw was her sickliness. All of us loved Felicity and all of us doted upon her, even the last-born of the family.

The youngest was Foster. Finally my father had the boy he had always wanted. Of course as the youngest he was spoiled and something of a scallywag, full of jokes and devilish tricks that only served to endear him even further in Father's eyes. But he wasn't quite as sharp as his sisters.

So this was our family of four girls, one boy and myself.

My story next.

Chapter 4

My name is Millicent Submit White, but mostly I'm called Millie. It's hard for me to describe how I belong to this family because I don't know all the details, only those that slip out without warning or that I've been able to pick up from quiet conversations I strain to overhear.

I was born to a village girl who couldn't keep me and begged Mother to take me. Since Mother was already well along with Felicity she thought that if she could remain in seclusion she could present both babies as hers. My father must have agreed to the plan so Felicity and I were presented as fraternal twins. Mother once told me that Millicent Submit was my given name, and I held onto it like a treasure as it was all I had to connect me to my birth mother except my dark brown hair and brown eyes.

I discovered my parents' deception when I overheard them one evening in the parlor. I was ten years old. I felt part of the family as a twin and had already been carrying a heavy share of the chores.

"Can we afford to send Millie to finishing school?" Mother sounded hopeful.

"No, no, that wasn't our plan. We need her to help run the inn. Remember that's what we agreed to when we took her in. I know she's a dear, but we can't afford it."

"Oh, but she's just such a bright young thing." Mother still sounded hopeful.

"Yes, but we need to think of our children first."

Our children? I was shocked.

I surprised myself when I walked into the parlor and boldly fixed my attention on Father's face, then Mothers. Both looked guilty.

"What does that mean? Think of *your* children first?" Father looked ashamed for a second, then angry.

"What were you doing listening to us?" He was stern.

"Am I not one of your children?"

"You are a dear part of our family, Millie, and we love you very much." Mother tried to soothe me. Father still seemed indignant.

"But," Mother continued, "come here and sit down. Let's talk." I stood my ground.

"I'm not one of your children?" I asked more feebly. Mother moved to one side of the settee and patted it for me to sit next to her, and when I did she took my hand.

"We feel like you're part of our family, but no, we took you in as a baby."

I was still in shock, all of the implications flashing through my mind. *Felicity was not my twin.*

"Felicity?" I asked. Mother shook her head. "Freda and Fairy?" She shook her head again. "Foster? Father?"

"No. Well, not by birth, but we love you, and to us you are very much part of the family."

"What happened?" So much was confusing.

"We took you in as a tiny infant; your mother couldn't keep you. Her father took her away. We told her we would keep you. She named you Millicent but her father said it was Millicent Submit." Mother hugged me.

I didn't know what to say.

"We didn't want to tell you because we were afraid it would trouble you. Your sisters don't know, nor does Foster. It's up to you if you want them to, but it must be a secret among us." She paused for a long time, watching my reaction.

"We love you, Millie. Never forget that."

There had been no formal adoption. The only paper filed was a birth record stating I was theirs. I thought later that my father, a wise man, realized I would offer another set of hands to help his hard-working wife at the inn and so I became one of the family. People taking in babies was not too uncommon, even taking them in without any formal papers. Nor was it uncommon to take in a maiden aunt or mother-in-law. It was what families did.

"But then, aren't I as much part of the family as the others? Shouldn't I go to finishing school too?"

Father looked at Mother with a pained expression. "Let's see what happens when the time comes. Perhaps we'll have enough to send everyone." He sounded hopeful, but somehow I was not.

I've often heard the story of Felicity's birth retold with my birth added on. Mother was set up in the second floor corner room with lots of windows and light. She went into labor on a warm May evening and "we" were not born until morning, with the sunlight streaming in and gracing us, red and wrinkled, with a warm glow. Mother says that Father had bouquets of daffodils placed around the room and it smelled of spring and new babies. Mother has recited the same story so many times that even she sometimes forgets that I was not born that day. She explains that I was delivered first and was larger than Felicity and it was no wonder that Felicity is weak and sickly since the robust Millie was hogging all the space.

Father, as the larger-than-life head of the family, expected everyone to obey him, and for one reason or another everyone did. The two bossy girls, Freda and Fairy, were his little toadies, always agreeing with him and fawning over him. Fern seemed to obey him but wouldn't get caught when she didn't. Felicity was always good; disobedience was not in her nature. Foster didn't matter. If he disobeyed it was overlooked or considered boyish independence. Foster could do anything.

I remember those early years when I shared a room with my sister Felicity. We both had nice little beds with a small table between them to put our lamp on. Because our room was close to one of the large center chimneys we stayed warm on the cold winter nights. Early in our childhood we were allowed time to play house with our dolls, and sometimes we were expected to help fold napkins and later help set the table. Generally we were equals and treated much the same except that more than anyone else Felicity would be sick and spend a day or a week in her bed. She and I had permission to walk to the store only a few doors away and sometimes we were given a penny to buy candy or an ice cream cone.

Before we started school Fern would spend time teaching us our alphabet and numbers and how to read simple words. Did I know how lucky I was? No. Now looking back at my early childhood I realize it was a simple and easy way to start my life. I felt I belonged in the family; I was lulled by a sense of security. Will I ever know how my life would have turned out if I had had a more difficult early youth? My wonderful life transformed itself slowly. Like a lobster in the pot of cold water oblivious to how hot the water is becoming, I didn't realize how my situation was changing. Even if I had, I wouldn't have known how to escape.

Chapter 5

At an early age I was helping out at the inn. I had been required to take on simple chores like folding towels and dusting. Not serious dusting where I might damage some fancy trinket but dusting chair rungs and table legs and empty tabletops or those with unbreakables on them. Chores close to the floor were favorites to assign me since I was short enough and nimble enough to sweep under the table or dust under the cabinet. The inn was a place where all of us were required to help to some degree. Still I was allowed to play and sometimes given special treats. When Mother gave me a cookie after I swept up a broken pitcher Freda and Fairy complained until they were also given cookies.

I was able to help in the kitchen too, and was often sent to the root cellar to get carrots and potatoes for supper. I went out with a basket and because I was still small I would have to make five or six trips to get enough to feed not only our family but our guests also. The root cellar had a long dark stone passage and the candle I carried sometimes went out as I entered. That always frightened me because of the scurrying of mice and other creatures I imagined living there along with the spiders that found a ready supply of bugs and draped their webs copiously along the passage. By the end of my last trip I was no longer frightened because the scurrying had stopped and the webs that had caught on my hair had been brushed away.

Every year as I grew older I would assume more of the chores. I grew stronger and tougher while Felicity never seemed to thrive.

I helped with the Monday wash, which included scrubbing sheets from the beds of the guests and boarders. This was a nasty job because one would never know from whence the stains came. Mother always encouraged me and would secretly give me a special treat that Freda and Fairy would not know to badger her about. Sometimes Mother and I would laugh about the stains and make up silly stories about what might have caused them. Mother would bring out a kettle of fresh hot water to add to my tub and I would grate off a handful of soap flakes and let the whole brew soak. If the stains were particularly difficult we might add a little lye and let the sheets sit longer. Then I would scrub them on the washboard until they were clean. Even though I didn't do all of the washing my knuckles on Mondays were always red and raw. Mother would have Fairy or Freda carry the baskets of heavy wet laundry to the line and hang it; the baskets were too heavy for me and the lines too high to reach. If the weight of the laundry pulled a line too low they would take a long forked piece of wood to prop it up so the clothes wouldn't sweep the ground and get dirty.

When I was younger Freda and Fairy had to do the dishes because I might break some of the glass or china. But they always grumbled about it so Father, though unaccustomed to carpentry or any manual skill, fashioned a stool I could stand on to reach the sink. It was a grape box to which he added small feet, and even this seemed difficult for him; we could hear him in the barn cussing at the inanimate object he was working on. And so I was to help with the dishes too.

Freda and Fairy worked on our parents, seeking the privileges of the ladies they thought they were destined to be. Born into a popular, well-known family and of moderate means, they didn't think they should be made to do the menial chores required to run an inn. Like the rest of us Freda and Fairy entered school at six years of age. Their innate laziness, which our parents passed over as just a phase, was not ignored by the teachers long hardened to the shilly-shallies of pupils unwilling to do their lessons. Both girls brought home less than desirable report cards and each of them complained of the ill treatment and favoritism of their respective teachers. Father marched down to the school to request an accounting of the teachers' rationale for such unacceptable treatment of his dear daughters. The teachers, however, were not so easily cowed, noting that Fern had no troubles with her lessons. Father was confounded. How could his favorites have fallen so far from grace? The result was the princesses were required to work harder on their lessons and they bullied Fern with more veiled aggression than before. The little meannesses they had before saved exclusively for me–a furtive pinch, a foot thrust out to trip me, a small clump of hair "accidentally" ripped out–drove Fern further and further into her shell. Fern was tall and thin, but Freda and Fairy were almost as tall and more robust. I knew Fern's wiriness would serve her when she finally retaliated. And she was going to retaliate. I thought that sooner or later the angry little bomb building up in her would turn into a small family drama and with her poor luck she would probably appear to be the party at fault.

I liked Fern, but she was hard to warm up to and always seemed to keep me and everyone else at arm's length. Except Felicity, whom she, like everyone else, loved. When Felicity and I had a moment to talk I would ask her about Fern, and she would always say Fern was unfairly singled out because people viewed her as different when in reality she was just reserved. Fern was, she observed, not just book-smart; she had wisdom and the common sense that more learned people sometimes lack. She knew what was going on in the family and why, but she kept it all to herself and shared her insights only with Felicity. Occasionally when I was the victim of an injustice Fern would flash me a knowing look, but she would never say anything. Only at these moments did I experience the understanding that came from sharing a common history and enemy.

Felicity loved everyone, even Freda and Fairy, who she thought feigned toughness on the surface but were just frightened children at their core, frightened and fearful she said. Felicity would willingly help with the chores when she could. Mother and Felicity and I would sit together on Wednesday and mend clothing and sheets, darn socks, patch and repair clothes and sometimes work on a quilt Mother had started several years before. These were happy times for me. Mother would brew tea and scour the pantry for treats that had been hidden. We would sit quietly and talk about school. Then we would talk about what Father was doing at work, or what the neighbors were doing, what new fabric might have come into the store or new book at the library. Sometimes we would even gossip about the guests. This was the most fun but we all understood it was to be kept in the strictest confidence. We'd talk about how Mr. Braidy was going out in the evening and not coming back until after midnight, and how Miss Chesley had a light appetite except when it came to the fresh bread that she would polish off half a loaf at a time along with a large spoonful of butter. We'd plan for the summer when school was over and the out-of-towners visited the lake and how we would have to make extra-large suppers and breakfasts to accommodate them. All would be merry until one of the rough set would come in loud and brash and insulting and, cleverly making it seem accidental, pull my hair or jab me with a pencil (not frequently since they seldom handled a writing utensil). The rough ones were secretly mean to me and to Fern but still loved Mother and Felicity, who both were unassuming, kind and gentle.

Not until later did the roughness become clothed in a thin veneer of haughty politeness.

Chapter 6

Foster, as Fitzgerald White's youngest and only son, was spoiled and almost as lazy as Freda and Fairy. It was assumed he would inherit everything, including the inn, and perhaps slip into his father's shoes at the factory. But there was a problem: he wasn't as keen as the rest. Even Freda and Fairy were quicker, certainly as lazy but more clever. Because of their age advantage and because of a sympathy among them that I always imagined was due to his favored status, they colluded with him and helped him cover up shortcomings or mischievous doings, and he responded in kind. Having easily gotten away with minor misdeeds, all of them became more brazen.

As the oldest Freda was usually the ringleader, although occasionally Fairy had an inspired plot to aggrieve an outsider. If Foster was involved he would go along, and that pleased them as it had the benefit of giving their plan some weight. Often he was unable to understand what they were planning or why. His bent being more towards silly pranks, he had not risen to the duo's level of meanness and Fairy would exaggeratedly roll her eyes in exasperation at his boyish innocence. The two gradually grew to realize that his priorities differed from theirs. His quest for fun was what drove his devilishness; hurting someone was not the point, but if that did happen it was unintentional, an unavoidable side effect.

But Freda and Fairy found some perverse pleasure in the hurt they could inflict.

Fern and I could not appeal to our parents to intervene since the tightly-bound trio stood up for one another. After trying once or twice, we were considered troublemakers ourselves. So Fern, Felicity and I had become a team to hold their evil in check. We saw ourselves as the good girls and took self-righteous pride in being kind, fair and not vindictive.

What started out as mean little physical hurts by those damsels of distress blossomed slowly into less direct and more inspired efforts at maliciousness. I believed that Fairy was the instigator in a plot to ruin a library book Fern had taken out. While Fern was out of the room someone pasted half a dozen of the book's pages together. When Fern found the damage she first flew into a rage, assuming she knew who had done the deed. She brought the book to Mother, hinting that her sisters were the transgressors. But Mother insisted that none of her children would ever do something like that. Once Fern realized that no one would be blamed or chastised she fell into despair. Her world of books, her escape from mundane day-to-day small town life, was under siege. Fairy could not have thought up a more cruel attack on Fern than damaging one of her books. To Fern books were more important than food. They were her food, her passion, her refuge. And Fairy had invaded it. Fern came to our room and sat with the book, slowly opening the pages, trying to unstick the damaged ones but tearing one instead. She started to cry, hugging the book to her chest. Felicity and I both tried to console her but she only cried harder, rocking to and fro. Fern, who was so often cloaked in her quiet reserve, was crumbling before our eyes.

I could hardly imagine what pleasure the wicked ones were deriving from this trick. Felicity and I were determined to discover who had instigated this and carried it out. But how? We had not been faced with this type of cruelty before and we were not sure how to approach it. Should one of us pretend to be with them and see if someone would let her guard down? I suspected they were too shrewd for that, perhaps anticipating this might be the ploy we would use to gather information. But what else could we do? Certainly Foster was the weak link. We might try to trick him.

And that was what I did.

Several days later when I found him alone, I told him that when I was cleaning his room I had come across an empty paste jar and I thought it was the one he'd used to glue Fern's book together. He blanched, and that told me that even though he may not have done it he knew about it. I threatened to tell Mother what he'd done and then she would tell Father, who so far was ignorant of the book defacement. I assured him Freda and Fairy would not stand behind him if it meant they would also be implicated. He answered that they were his sisters and would certainly stand with him. But I made him question the loyalty of the other two and stressed how serious it was to deface a library book. He tried to leave but I blocked his path. I told him he had also hurt Fern, who had cried over it. Now he was getting more nervous.

"I didn't do it!" he finally exclaimed.

"But you know who did, don't you?" He nodded.

"Tell me and I won't tell Mother you were involved."

He looked cornered, ready to give up.

"Fairy, Fairy did it. It was her idea and she did it." He started to cry.

"Okay. Don't worry. I won't tell Mother."

He looked relieved but then also fearful.

"But what about Fairy and Freda? They will be mad that I told you and they'll want to get me too."

"Don't worry about them. I won't let those girls know. This will be our secret, right?" He nodded again, and looked more relieved.

Once he'd told me I decided that perhaps Felicity, Fern and I should handle this together. It seemed to us our sisters thought themselves above reproach and no one could impress upon them how much pain they caused. They might be able to wheedle their way out of difficulties when our parents were involved but we would find a way to bring them to justice. But in the end Felicity and I didn't have to. Fern did it herself.

"And remember," I told Foster in a parting shot, "Fern says that karma will get you in the end." He looked at me fearfully.

"Who's Karma?"

"She says that's some kind of mystical fate that means if you do something bad it will come back to get you, and if you do something good it will also come back to you. Fern knows these things because she reads a lot."

Foster's eyes got big. "Geez, really? But I didn't do it myself. Does it still count?"

"Yup. It counts because you didn't stop her."

His shoulders drooped as he walked away knowing that somewhere, sometime, Karma was going to get him.

Chapter 7

The evening after I talked to Foster I told Felicity what I had found out. She was upset at the meanness of her sisters. She had been willing to believe that perhaps they were not involved, that maybe the pages were stuck together when Fern took the book from the library, but now the truth was out. Yet she still had difficulty believing it was done from meanness, hoping it was just a devilish prank. I loved Felicity. Everyone did. I loved her innocence, her kindness, her unfailing belief in the goodness of others. But this time I was frustrated with her naiveté. I told her we should be the ones to handle a response to this and she should remember how important books were to Fern and how Fern had cried on her shoulder. I reminded her how deliberate an attack this had been to hurt our Fern, and she finally agreed that we should do something to correct the wrong. But neither of us had an idea as to what, so we decided to wait and think about how to go about it. We were not sure whether to tell Fern, but finally we thought it best.

While we mulled over our plans for revenge, plotting slowly and deliberately, Fern and I particularly savoring the many impossible and silly strategies, events took a strange twist.

Foster and some of his friends had been playing on the penstocks[1] that fed Woods Mill. It was during the hot dry spell and the boys were trying to cool off without going to the lake for a swim. The wooden penstocks sprayed water where they leaked and often kids would run under the spray, or climb onto the penstocks and run along them until the building manager yelled at them. This was one of those days when the leader of their little troupe, a rough and loud braggart named Stanley, was running along a penstock. Foster, wanting to be one of the bold fellows, did the same but with nowhere near the elegant step of Stanley. They got to a spot where a fine spray was spouting up and coating the wood with a green slime. Stanley, ever the showoff, continued on as though this was a challenge tailor-made for him. As he hopped forward with a firm jump his foot broke through the penstock's rotting wood, and the ensuing geyser of water threw him into a stone piling that held up the wooden pipe. Watching in disbelief, Foster lost his balance and fell the five feet to the ground, his school pants catching on a loose board that tore a gaping hole and cut him. Foster grabbed the tear of clothing and ran over to Stanley, who was lying motionless on the ground. The other boys started to gather around and one of them ran to the mill. The foreman came out cussing loudly.

"I've told you boys a thousand times to keep away from the penstocks. Dammit. I knew this would happen sooner or later."

---

[1] A penstock is a large enclosed pipe that delivers water to a turbine or water wheel. Early penstocks were made of wood.

He walked over to inspect Stanley, whose lower leg was bent out at an impossible angle. The foreman carried him semi-conscious and moaning into the mill, where he started screaming. Foster and his pals had followed the foreman to the door, and he motioned for them to stay outside. They waited, all looking sheepishly at each other. Foster was now noticing the cut and bruise on his leg, which was starting to throb.

Dr. Mason came down the street, his sleek horse trotting quickly in front of his trim buggy, and wasted no time hopping out and handing the reins to one of the boys. He grabbed his black bag and entered the factory, ignoring the rest of the boys hovering near the door.

Finally Stanley's parents arrived. His father carried him out, limp and pale and looking much smaller than the other boys remembered him, his leg heavily bandaged. The boys headed home.

Foster knew he had to go home but dreaded it. Torn pants, cut leg, and news that had probably already reached his family.

"Karma," he said to the other kids. "Karma will get you if you're not good." They looked at him blankly.

"What's that?"

"It's fate. Karma. You know, what you do comes back to haunt you." His tone was knowing.

Foster went to the inn's storeroom door and snuck up the back stairs to our room. I was in the first-floor washroom doing chores but Felicity was sitting by the window in our room, darning socks. She took one look at him and knew something was wrong.

"Karma got me, Felicity," was all he said before he fainted and fell to the floor.

Felicity, of course frightened, ran to him and touched his forehead. His eyes flickered. She ran down the back stairs and told me to go up to our room while she went to brew some tea.

I found him sitting in a chair, leaning against the dresser and holding his leg.

"I was playing with Stanley and the guys down by Woods Mill. I hurt myself and tore my pants." He gave me a pathetic look and pointed at his leg.

I bent to see the damage. A bad scrape, a bruise and a cut that looked serious but not so serious that it would require more than a good bandage. On my way to the kitchen I passed Felicity as she brought a small pot of tea upstairs.

When I returned with a warm washcloth, bandages and mercurochrome I found Foster sitting with his leg up. He whimpered, "Felicity's gone to get another pair of pants from my room. I'm going to be in such trouble! These are my school pants."

Felicity came back and Foster changed into the old pair of pants she offered.

I started to wash his leg and he flinched but didn't say anything. When I put the mercurochrome on he cried out but I blew on it, trying to take away the sting. I covered the wound with a bandage and pulled the pant leg down.

Felicity busied herself with a needle and thread trying to mend his pants.

"I think we can make these almost as good as new. I can probably wash off the green stains too. You are lucky you weren't hurt more seriously. What happened?"

At this he shuddered.

"Stanley and I were climbing on the penstocks at Woods Mill. Stanley broke through and was thrown to the ground. He was hurt pretty bad—I think he has a broken leg because it was all crooked and stuff. When he fell off I slipped too."

We both looked at him in dismay, shaking our heads. Foster's eyes welled up.

"Do you think I'm going to get in trouble? Do we have to tell Mom and Dad?"

Felicity and I looked at each other and one of her eyebrows went up. We were so close that I could almost read her mind. Should we torment this fellow further? Should we frighten him, make him pay? We both knew this was not Felicity's way, but it did cross our minds.

"What do you think, Millie?"

"Well, he was doing something he should not have been doing, and he hasn't been the best of brothers lately. What do you think, Felicity?" Foster's eyes went back and forth between us trying to discern which way we were going to go.

"Foster, what do you think we should do?" Felicity was prolonging the questioning and seemed to be enjoying it. Foster looked at the floor.

"I suppose I should tell them myself."

Unable to bear his sad countenance Felicity patted him on the head.

"Listen, this time we won't say anything, but I hope you've learned a lesson." He looked up hopefully.

"I have. I've learned to stay off the penstocks, not to try to copy Stanley and to be good or Karma will get me."

Chapter 8

After the penstock accident Foster was kinder to the three of us, and especially to Fern. He also gave a wider berth to Freda and Fairy, who seemed to understand there had been a shift. But rather than being concerned they were now picking on him in addition to the rest of us, but wisely, not as much.

For our part, Fern, Felicity and I accepted him into our little group of kinder family members. But even though we outnumbered them we felt powerless against the "mean sisters."

Our dear mother detected a subtle change, but said nothing.

This was when Fern struck. Her plan, unbeknownst to the rest of us, showed genius.

Her day came at the end of the school year when she was awarded a prize for creative writing. To honor all the prizewinners the school invited them and their family members to an evening event to receive the awards and also read from their award-winning work. Fern had won first place. The whole family attended along with many other families in town.

The fourth, third and second place winners rose in turn to accept their prize and read their work. When it was Fern's turn we all stood up and gave her a rousing ovation, embarrassing her but affording us a great deal of satisfaction.

It wasn't until part-way through her reading that Freda and Fairy realized they were the villains in Fern's story.

At each outburst from the audience they sank further and further down into their seats until finally Freda got up and stormed out, causing another gale of laughter from the crowd as Mother followed.

Fairy stayed put but didn't stand up with the audience when Fern finished reading to hearty applause.

Back at home Mother and Father said not a word to Fern about the mockery in the story. She had won an award and they congratulated her.

There was quiet discussion in the parlor that evening. Apparently Freda and Fairy were getting a lesson in sibling cooperation.

They ignored Fern for almost a month, responding to her with cold civility only when they couldn't avoid it.

Summer was bearing down upon our village. Visitors were making reservations and coming in by train. Our busiest season had begun.

I often had to help people carry their bags to their rooms, sometimes up two flights of stairs and down the long hall. When Father was home he would assist but when they arrived during the work day much of it fell to me, though sometimes Fern helped.

All manner of folks visited. Middle-aged ladies enjoyed being rowed around the lake in style with a parasol and the promise of a picnic at the end. Elderly gentlemen with large moustaches and gold pocket watches desired the newspaper delivered to their door in the morning, requiring me to run to the store for extra copies so the grand fellows could read them before breakfast. At times whole families came, or just mothers and their children, who were always excited to be able to go swimming. Sometimes there were serious fishermen, and Mother asked them to use the storeroom entrance and stay on the third floor near the stairs, leaving their paraphernalia in the storeroom so that "all manner of mud and nature wouldn't be dragged through the halls." They were always required to arrive at meals presentable and not in their sport-fishing attire. Occasionally a musician would come and play for us in the evening after supper. Or an artist would appear with wooden cases of paints and a wooden easel contraption that looked much like a medieval machine with levers and knobs and hooks and bolts. Sometimes lovers would arrive, newly married and obviously infatuated. Mother always insisted on waiting on them herself, being sure to offer them breakfast served in their rooms with flowers on the tray. She'd put them in a spot behind the parlor she called the quiet room, so, she said, they wouldn't be disturbed, but we guessed it was so they wouldn't disturb anyone else.

We kept a coop of chickens and before breakfast I would bring them food and water and collect the eggs. Breakfast was served at eight to give our guests time to freshen up and dress after waking. Sometimes the fishermen went out early and came back for breakfast. If we were lucky they would bring fish and share with us so we could offer a nice bass supper, for which Father gave them several pints.

Mother, Fern, Felicity and I prepared breakfast starting the night before, making bread dough oven-ready for the morning so the dining room would be sweet with the welcoming smell of baking bread. We usually served meat, either bacon or sausage or hash, along with pancakes, eggs, and oatmeal or cream of wheat. Freshly baked beans often provided a pleasant change. We ground coffee the night before and brewed up a large percolator full. Tea was available with sugar and heavy cream. Butter, bought fresh from the farm on Friday, was offered for the warm bread along with preserves put up the previous fall. We did as much as we could the evening before so that nothing was late for breakfast. Although we served a variety of good food it was not in the greatest abundance, and late arrivers did not find the selection that earlier ones did.

Felicity and I set up the long breakfast tables the evening before, one or two depending upon the number of guests. We would often have fifty or sixty napkins for the Monday wash day, and the chore I enjoyed as a child because of the ease of folding became an annoyingly long drill as I grew older. If we had a large number of guests we had to launder sheets at least twice a week, sometime even more frequently. All the girls helped wash dishes but of course Freda and Fairy would complain and moan the whole time. What could have been a pleasant task with the family became a difficult chore we all dreaded, but without them it would have taken an hour longer.

Once dishes were done and put away and soiled linens collected and brought to the laundry room, we swept the dining room and parlor with the new German carpet sweeper we'd just gotten that was very efficient at picking up crumbs and dust. Then we would sweep the kitchen and wash the floor.

After the guests left for the day I made their beds and swept their rooms, hanging and straightening up towels on their washstands. I'd bring a bucket of water to each room to refill their water pitcher, and empty their wash basin into a second bucket and then wipe the basin clean.

Next I'd sweep the halls.

My other job, the most nasty and disliked of them all, was to empty the "thundermugs," a slang Mother used for the chamber pots. I would dump them into a bucket and empty that into the outhouse, then rinse out and dry the pots, replace the covers and push them back under the beds. I always hoped the pot would be empty or contain only pee, but occasionally an unsavory stew greeted me.

I probably went up and down the stairs fifty times a day. All of this served to build me into a sturdy young lady, but Felicity still seemed to get weaker.

Doctors diagnosed her with iron-poor blood and prescribed different vitamins. She sometimes improved for a while, only to slip back into lethargy, covering her little coughs with her handkerchief. Yet she was always willing to help with the chores without complaint.

Supper was served at seven, starting with bread from the morning baking and a soup or stew. Potatoes and whatever vegetables were in season accompanied a turkey or roast. Dessert of pie or cake finished it off.

The family ate in the kitchen on a sturdy table that served as our work table and then our dinner table. A large kitchen stove was kept going all day and part of the evening, fed by wood we had delivered monthly. In the summer

months cooking could be uncomfortably hot. Most
vegetables were stored in the root cellar cooled by ice cut
during the winter that was kept covered in straw and sawdust.
A spacious pantry housed our baking and cooking
paraphernalia, and a china and linen closet held plates,
silverware and dining needs. An enormous double sink under
the window (where I got my first bath) was big enough to
soak almost twenty place settings, the first tub for washing
and the second for rinsing.

We were lucky to have a hand pump over the sink so
no one had to go out to the well to bring in water, but we had
to use a bucket to fill a gigantic kettle to set on the stove
several times a day. The reservoir on the stove also needed
to be filled.

The tasks of running the inn were endless. While I
welcomed the summer with its warm sunny green days, the
amount of work it brought was almost crushing. Gradually
the burden was piled on me. Year after year my duties grew,
more and more chores from the time I woke until the time I
rolled into bed exhausted. No days off, no freedom, no
wages, no friends outside the family, no sunshine other than
hanging clothes or during a quick walk to the store. Yet I
hardly knew what I was missing. I could see only the guests
we cared for and how they fared, sensing that in many cases
I wasn't in their social class so I could never attain the
freedom they enjoyed. The rest of the family worked hard
enough to make me feel I was not the only laborer. Freda
and Fairy escaped most of the housekeeping with the
unspoken reason, understood by all, that they were to be
ladies and marry local gentry, and to prepare for that they

needed to learn the more ladylike skills of art and entertaining unburdened by our daily workload.

Chapter 9

My life started to go awry when Freda finally had the audacity and meanness to attack Felicity.

On a warm summer evening we were gathered in the kitchen after supper, our regular chores done. Fern was sitting in a rocking chair near the west window to make the most of the evening light as she read her book. Fairy sat at the table fussily manicuring her nails. Felicity was near her darning socks; she had a talent for repairing them so well the owner could hardly see or feel where the holes had been. I was polishing a couple of silver serving pieces to use in the dining room the next day. Foster was outside and I could hear him bouncing a rubber ball rhythmically against the woodshed. Mother and Father were in the parlor with the guests fulfilling their social duties. I heard Father laughing loudly at his own joke and asking one of the men if he wanted a refill.

As she normally did Freda came stumping down the stairs like a herd of buffalo. She threw open the door with such force that Felicity started. Somehow this annoyed Freda and she marched over and slapped Felicity's hand.

"Oh, stop being such a timid mouse!" And out the kitchen door she went.

Felicity jumped up, dropping the socks and spool of thread. She stood there shocked, her hand out with the needle sticking deep into her finger. It all happened so fast we took several seconds to react.

I grabbed her hand and pulled out the needle. Felicity screamed and put the finger to her mouth. Everyone else sat stunned, not fully realizing what had happened, not knowing what to do. I grabbed a clean towel and handed it to Felicity, then ran to the root cellar and broke off a piece of ice with the icepick. Running back I put the ice on her finger. It was still bleeding a little.

"Press the ice hard against it and the bleeding will stop." She did, and it did.

"Come upstairs. I'll make you some tea and bring it up to you." I didn't know what else to do. Should we sit there as though nothing had happened? Or make a scene and call in our parents? Or go out after Freda and confront her?

Felicity went up to our bedroom and I poured some hot water from the always-simmering kettle into one of the little pots that had a small spoon of tea leaves in the ball. I took a tray, some milk, sugar and a couple of biscuits and headed up the backstairs after Felicity. No one moved or said anything.

It was another one of those events that is etched into my mind, those few minutes. When I looked back Fern was watching me, lips parted as if to say something, book still poised open. Fairy was still holding her nail buffer mid-swipe. I just turned and ascended the stairs with the tray.

I pushed open the door with the tray and found Felicity sitting by the window holding the ice and towel on her finger. I set the tray down by her and took her hand and looked at the wound. The bleeding had stopped but it was red where the needle had gone in.

"Put the ice back on it. I'll get some alcohol and a bandage." She obeyed and I went for the bandages. When I returned I poured tea, put sugar and milk in it and handed her the cup. She released the towel and quietly took the cup. As I started to wipe alcohol on the site of the injury she drew in a sharp breath. I bandaged it and sat down across from her, the fading light illuminating the room with a rosy hue.

"I'm not a timid mouse, am I?" I saw a tear start to run down her cheek. She wiped it with the back of her hand.

I voiced the first silly thing that came to mind.

"I love mice." But as I said it I was already plotting revenge, a thousand tortures for Freda, the meanest person I knew. I could only think then of what revenge I wanted to take, but I was too consumed by anger to find a suitable method. I knew I needed time to concoct a worthwhile plan. I knew I should cool down and keep my wits about me. My anger with this girl, now almost a woman, had hit a dangerous threshold.

Felicity, so guileless, was tired and ready to let go of it. But if she was the mouse, I was the tigress whose teeth Freda could never have imagined were so sharp. All of her transgressions had piled up and ran through my mind like a millwheel, round and round, over and over.

I didn't sleep well that night. I could hear Felicity's quiet breathing in the next bed, but all I could think about was her pain and the many shades of revenge.

Chapter 10

I had become obsessed with Freda. I watched her and listened to her and saw the selfish way she went through life. In some ways her self-absorption made me sad. How could anyone be so oblivious to the feelings of other people? I almost thought that she needed no punishment, that she was probably very lonely flying around in her small little orbit with only the likes of Fairy to shine on her. But then I thought if I did nothing she would never realize how she impacted the world around her, and she should, I decided, be made aware. Maybe then she would have a chance to turn her life around and become a better person. I felt as though I would be doing her a favor, that I was her judge, on the moral high ground, and I was going to help her.

While I observed Freda, looking deeper for her strengths and weaknesses that I might exploit, I was also more aware of Felicity. To me she was the exact opposite of Freda. She was thoughtful and kind and gentle and tactful. How could the two of them come from the same parents, or be raised in the same family? I couldn't fathom it.

Wanting to do something special for Felicity, I surprised Father by asking if there was an odd job I could do at the box factory to earn a little money. He thought about it for a while and then explained that they needed me helping at the inn and didn't know if they could spare me. I told him it would just be long enough to save three dollars and then I would quit and not seek full-time employment. After some deliberation he agreed, saying they had a boy who was going away for a month so I could come in for a few hours a day in the afternoon and paste labels on cartridge boxes. The boy would return and want his job back. He could give me the three dollars for the month. I thanked him and assured him he wouldn't be disappointed; I could do my work at the inn and the factory work as well.

So it began. I would rush through my regular chores, help prepare supper, gobble it down and help clean up, then hurry to the box factory, which happily was only a quick ten-minute walk from the inn. Fortunately it was summer and the work continued into the evening as long as the light lasted, so with brush and gluepot I pasted labels. The labels were for special target-shooting cartridges and were ornate, picturing an eagle. I became very proficient at the job. When I got home for the evening I helped with preparations for the next day's breakfast, then collapsed into bed exhausted.

Everyone knew I had this additional job and I understood it was occasionally a topic of discussion. Why would Millie want to work even more than she already did? What would she do with the money? I think my parents were concerned that I was seeking independence and might not want to work at the inn once I found I could earn real money for my time. I was not paid for all my labors there. No one was; it was just expected of us. We were lucky, Father once said when annoyed at someone's griping, that we had a good roof over our heads and plenty of food to eat.

I was the hardest worker at home. I knew I wasn't a full-fledged White even though I carried the name. It was evident in so many ways, including my physique. I was an averaged-sized person but trim and strong with dark brown hair and brown eyes. Even though I was approaching puberty I had no obvious signs of breasts. The other Whites had thick auburn hair and most were tall with the exception of Felicity, who was in all ways smaller than the rest. The other girls were becoming buxom. Even the lean Fern had respectable breasts and the wide White hips, but a flat derriere. Sometimes they teased me good-naturedly about my more masculine shape, calling me "the other White boy." So even though I lived as part of the family I knew in my heart I would never be a full member; I would never be blood. What would happen to me once I reached adulthood? Would I still be working at the inn? Would I be expected to marry and move on with my life? It wasn't as apparent to me as it was for the others. The White girls were expected to marry well, to find eligible bachelors in town or from neighboring towns. Fern thought she would like to go to college if they would let her. It was assumed that Foster would inherit the inn. But what of Millie? What would happen to Millie? Mother once spoke of my marrying a nice mill boy, and there were a couple of them Father invited to a picnic as a special reward to the millworkers. They had looked nervously at the other White girls and shyly at me, but at my young age I had no thought of marriage or boys.

So even though there seemed to be no future plans for me they couldn't do without my help at the inn. The rough girls groused they had too much work to do, and Fern did the work but complained it took time away from her books. Either singly or with my work split out between them, the loss of my housekeeping would have been irreplaceable, or at least that was what I thought.

I stayed at the box factory for the month Father had offered and when the boy came back I was given not the three dollars we had agreed upon but FOUR dollars! Father said I had so far surpassed the work of the other paste boys that he was sad to see me go. He also expressed his gratitude for my help at the inn, and his rare compliment was enough to make me want to stay forever.

I knew exactly what I was going to purchase with my riches. I had seen it at Wellwood's several months back. Tucked in the glass cabinet with the fancy shears and sewing doo-dads was a fine silver thimble. It was quite expensive but I had saved enough to pay for it and still have a little I could set aside. The shopkeeper put it in a small velveteen pouch that he said came with it, and likely because of the cost of the item he threw in a packet of needles and a pin cushion. I was very excited to have made such a good purchase. I expected that Felicity would be pleased with the gift. Such a fine mender of clothes should have a special tool of the trade.

All the while I had been working at the box factory and focusing on my surprise for Felicity I had not forgotten Freda, but the obsession had subsided for a while.

I watched her sashay around the dining table as we set it for breakfast. Her exaggerated swinging of her hips and pushing out of her chest reminded me of some Gibson girl pictures I'd seen in the magazines she left lying around, although she was not able to cinch up her waist to the hourglass figure they had. She was becoming a woman and flaunting it to no one but her family members. Mother watched her and just shook her head, so silly was her exaggerated posture. Fairy tried to mimic her but had not quite mastered the confident air that Freda managed to carry about herself.

I was beginning to think this would be her weak point, her belief she was somehow glamorous. But in reality she was slightly ridiculous. This was Coventry for goodness sake, not New York City.

What would I do? It came to me in a flash when I heard we were going to have a picnic for some of Father's friends and their families. Father was trying to bring attention to his eligible daughters, hoping to plant a seed in the minds of some of the more respected parents. An elegant picnic might be the perfect venue.

Chapter 11

Several days prior to the picnic I watched as my sisters started to work themselves up into a fever at the thought of the several prominent visitors and their families. They knew there were young men in the group and this might be as close to a "coming out" as they might ever have.

Father had ordered some special provisions for the event including a small keg of beer and a suckling pig that the baker would roast for us.

Since the picnic was to be held at the inn during the weekend it would be almost a public event. The boarders and guests would be attending so we all had to participate in the preparation and serving.

Even the preparation was festive. Father ordered Chinese lanterns hung from wires in the yard and lit with tea lights.

We'd cleaned more thoroughly than normal, dusting areas that didn't usually get attention, washing, polishing, and waxing. The inn literally shone. Father had some of the men who worked for him paint the yard chairs and benches.

As the big day approached, the house was in a tizzy. My sisters were wound as tight as springs.

The day dawned bright and beautiful, and we rushed through breakfast so we could start getting ready. Father had the boys from the mill set up sawhorses with boards across them to make tables in the yard and Mother brought the tablecloths out to cover them so we wouldn't see the sawhorse legs. It was already starting to look elegant.

We hard-boiled eggs and deviled them. We cooked chicken and made chicken-salad finger sandwiches. Father had the butcher carve the pig and we planned to serve it on great silver platters, alongside baked rolls, pickles, and potato salad. This was going to be a banquet fit for a king.

A separate table was set up for plates, utensils and napkins, and another for glasses by the beer. Father rolled the keg to the entrance of the root cellar where it would stay cool, set it on a block of ice and tapped it. Sampling the brew (which after the agitation was mostly foam) he declared it "delightful." Another fellow from the mill was to come to serve the beer.

As the sun rose we were grateful for the perfect weather but also for the large maples shading our little affair. Between several of them Father and Foster ran wires to the shed and then to the house. From these they hung the Chinese lanterns, all ready to be lit but as equally festive during the day.

Everyone was excited. Felicity, unusually animated, was helping with the preparations, dancing around with Foster and with me. When she followed me into root cellar I expected some kind of prank but she pushed me onto the saw-dusted ice, pressed up against me and kissed me on the lips, then grabbed my hand and ran back out onto the lawn and danced around some more. I was embarrassed and pulled away. "I've got to get that basket of lemons. I'll be back." Normally I would enjoy her exuberance, but the kiss had unnerved me. She watched me with disappointment but went off to the kitchen to find, she said, more glasses for the table.

Our usually quiet yard looked like a circus or a fair. As the excitement rose so did the tension and some of the family sniped and griped. Father said he had no patience with that today and told them to behave or they would not be allowed to join the party. Of course it was Freda and Fairy who had occasioned this rebuke, and quickly quiet down they did.

A gigantic bowl of deep red punch with fruit and a large chunk of ice floating in it finished off the grand display. The ice made me flash to Felicity earlier in the root cellar. It rattled me.

Preparations completed, the girls all ran upstairs to dress and primp. With a little of my earnings I had purchased a large pink ribbon and some rouge, and unbeknownst to the others I had traded for a second-hand dress that was the most beautiful piece of clothing I had ever owned and fit me acceptably well.

Through the open window we heard the first guests walking on the sidewalk by the river, hailing each other gaily. Our parents were greeting them and we could hear them wonder out loud where the girls were.

Freda and Fairy rushed downstairs first, and as Felicity and I watched from our bedroom window our parents made a show of introducing them to everyone. The rough girls, on their best behavior, were most gracious.

Felicity was in awe of my new dress and helped me, gently brushing my hair and tying in the new ribbon. Each stroke reminded me of that kiss. That kiss. Was it just a sisterly kiss? Was I reading too much into it? It shook me.

When we went out all heads turned. We felt like the most beautiful girls at the ball, like Cinderella. We heard one man exclaim, "Ah, Fitzy, you saved the best for last," a comment that I'm sure upset several family members. We were introduced around to some of those my Father called "the better families in town." The boys shook our hands and gave us appreciative looks. One of them offered to get us some punch, another to bring us a plate from the table. The other boys were milling closer to us and making conversation. Had we been paddling on the lake? How did we like a certain teacher; had we had her yet? Felicity and I were overwhelmed.

None of this was lost on Father. Freda and Fairy were trying not to notice by talking with the parents of the more favored fellows. Fern went directly to her mathematics teacher, and appearing deep in discussion never left his side.

Father called to me across the yard. "Millie, shouldn't you pass around some of the punch?" I knew my plan had worked. The boys much preferred Felicity and me to the mean sisters and this obvious pitch to demean me was not going unnoticed.

"Of course, Father," was my sweet reply, and I hoisted a tray of glasses with poured punch and made the rounds to the boys and then their parents, refilled the tray and then served our family. When I got to Freda I tripped, tossing what was left of the punch all over her new pinafore.

There was a gasp. Everyone saw it. Freda in her usual manner reacted as expected. She slapped me hard across the face. Then she raced inside. It was worth getting a slap. What were the chances that this would not shock everyone at the event and by tomorrow be the gossip all over town? She would never get a boy in this town. She'd have to go shopping elsewhere. I picked up the tray and the glasses, several of which had broken, and brought it into the kitchen. Mother followed.

"What's going on, Millie? Did you do that deliberately?" She paused to wait for my reply but I busied myself with the glasses. "Is everything okay between you and Freda?"

I couldn't understand why she hadn't seen the problem years ago, why she hadn't seen what a little witch she'd raised, but this was not the time to work through years of abuse.

"No, I just tripped. I'm so sorry." I tried to sound truly contrite. Duplicity was getting easier.

She gave me a hug and went upstairs to help and comfort Freda.

I went back outside and started to pass around the finger sandwiches. Fairy wisely stayed clear of me. Felicity was now the shining belle of the ball. I knew that the glass slipper would never fit my foot.

Chapter 12

That evening after changing my clothes I began cleaning up all the dishes and napkins and silverware. The furniture was put away, the lanterns snuffed and folded. I had time to reflect on my action. Was I really trying to help Freda become a more caring person, or was I just trying to get revenge? I decided it was likely about revenge, not just for Felicity but for all the little pinches, the injustices, and the meannesses we all experienced at her hand.

Freda wasn't talking to me and by extension Fairy wasn't either. It was a quiet and subdued evening after all the hoopla of the buildup. Fern and I were doing the dishes.

Felicity sat by the stove quietly intent on her mending. Softly she said, "It was a strange day, wasn't it?"

I looked over my shoulder at her, and Fern, who had been helping me, paused to look too.

"I mean the day should have been a jolly success, but didn't it turn out oddly?" She looked up from her work and held my gaze for a second, and then I turned back to the sink.

I realized she suspected my mishap was deliberate and was disappointed in me. Fern and I continued to wash and wipe the dishes.

I could hear Father and Mother in the parlor talking in low voices. Every once in a while I heard my name and Freda's. I wanted so much to get closer to the door to listen to what they were saying.

"I liked what you did today," Fern murmured under her breath, casting a cautious glance at Felicity. I was so focused on the conversation in the parlor that I started when she spoke and almost dropped the plate I was washing.

"What do you mean?" I whispered. How could I feign innocence? Fern was one of "us" and I shouldn't play the dummy to her. Besides, she was smart enough to know what was going on.

"Really? You don't know what I mean?" She whispered back, insulted that I might think her so stupid.

"I had to. She deserved it. So many years of the nasties. When would I get another opportunity like that?" I had to speak the truth to someone and I knew Fern was solid and would not, even under duress, give my secret away.

"It was perfect," Fern whispered appreciatively. We went on washing and drying and stacking.

Felicity yawned loudly and folded up her work. "Well, I guess it's time for bed." It was awkward. She must have heard us whispering but didn't know what to make of it. I'd never been secretive around Felicity; we were too close. It seemed that a little schism had been wedged ever so gently between us. I was fearful that what I had hoped would avenge the hurt to her may have instead pushed her away.

The next day at supper we got the news. Freda was being sent to a special school for girls and young women in Farmington. At this her neck grew longer. Her nose slightly up in the air, she looked at each of us around the table and when she came to me she paused, with an expression of satisfaction that said, "See, I came out of this better than you." I just smiled back. Nothing could have pleased me more than to have her on the other side of the Connecticut River. Fairy would now need to smooth her feathers, maybe even become a nicer person.

Fairy smiled but looked a little nervous. What would she do without her evil mentor? Without someone to guide her in how to act she was a rudderless brat. Which way would she sail? Would she try to be the dominator, attempting to fill Freda's shoes? I doubted it. She was just Freda's stooge. Without Freda she would be a barnacle and latch onto the closest substitute. But who would it be?

After supper when we were clearing the table Father approached me and asked to speak to me in the parlor.

My heart sank. I dried my hands on my apron and followed him into the parlor, where Mother was already seated. He leaned one arm on the mantelpiece of the fireplace.

"We are not totally convinced that your accident yesterday was an accident," Father started. "Don't try to deny it as we would not have you lie further to try to fix the mistake." I looked down. They knew. Denying it would indeed make me seem more insulting to them.

"We know," Father continued, "that you and Freda have not always gotten along. We hoped that over time this would work itself out but since it hasn't we've decided that Freda should get away a little earlier than we'd planned. She is to learn some of the finer points of being a lady and this is a very nice school we are sending her to." He paused. "But what of you?" He looked at me, bending slightly to see my downturned eyes. I looked up.

"You have been a treasured member of our family. You know that, don't you?" I nodded my head and now was beginning to feel the shame I might have felt if Freda were a nicer person. This was a good family I had found myself in. I knew that a tear was about to run down my cheek.

"Actually, Millie, we don't know what we would have done without you all of these years." I sniffed back the tear.

"Your mother and I don't know what to do. We don't know what we would do without you but we need to be sure that you know your actions were more hurtful to us than you might have imagined." I nodded again, more tears starting down my cheeks.

"Are you determined to be more respectful and loving to all of us?"

"Yes." My voice was trembling.

"Okay now, go finish up your chores in the kitchen. And, by the way, we've decided to give all of the children small salaries according to their help at the inn. It won't be much but you should not feel the need to get another job. Okay?"

I felt so embarrassed. I rushed over to give him a hug, then went to Mother and gave her one. "Thank you. You are so kind to me." And I turned and went into the kitchen before I could shed any more tears.

Chapter 13

Fern saw my red and moist eyes but said nothing. I went about working on the dishes, applying the dishrag and towel as I never had before.

In a low voice Fern asked, "Is everything okay?" I just nodded and went back about my business.

I could feel changes happening around me in the next few months. Freda was acting even more haughty that before, her mean nature being gradually replaced by a superior one. Though not as nasty or impolite as she had been, she was now cold and sullen.

Mother took her on the train to Willimantic to purchase a wardrobe. And in the months before she went away she seemed to lose what our parents called her baby fat and change into a woman before our eyes. The overly feminine wags of her hips were toned down and the exaggerated pushing up of her breasts was relaxed. Mother's efforts to instruct her the requirements of being a lady in polite society seemed to be making an impression.

I for one felt that the tension among the women of the house had calmed and the atmosphere was overall more pleasant. Freda and I avoided each other and spoke only if absolutely necessary. Fairy was the one who seemed most impacted by the changes.

Freda had distanced herself from Fairy, who seemed lost and started to spend more time with Felicity and me. Finally one evening at the dinner table she cracked. While

Freda was talking in her new superior tone about the latest fashions in New York and Paris Fairy dropped her fork, put her head in her hands and started to sob. Of course everyone turned to her, curious about the reason for her outburst. Jumping up from the table she ran to the stairs and up to her bedroom. Mother put her napkin on the table and followed.

After at least fifteen minutes both came back, sat down at the table and finished supper. Fairy didn't look at anyone. Mother joined in the conversation as though nothing had happened. Fern and I both raised our eyebrows, exchanging a glance that said "I can't wait to find out what's going on."

The clean-up after supper included only Fern, Felicity and me. The mean girls were summoned into the parlor with our parents. Later we found out that Fairy was also promised finishing school once she got a little older. In the meantime Freda was to take her under her wing and show her some of the finer points of being a lady. As though, I thought, Freda would know.

A week later Father took Fern into the parlor and the result was that Fern, who had been learning to work the front desk and keep the inn's books, was to be taken on at the mill in the accounting department. There she would be trained and perhaps one day assume some of the mill's bookkeeping duties. Father said if she excelled and wanted to go he would try to get her a place at the academy where she could learn to become an accountant.

Felicity and I had no visits to the parlor. I decided it was because Felicity, so pretty and sweet, would find herself a good husband among the more established families in town, and I imagined they expected me to continue on working at the inn, perhaps marrying and bringing my husband on board also. There was no glass slipper in my future, no upper-crust charm school. I wasn't hurt. Somewhere in me was the knowledge that I had been groomed for this all my life. But I had no idea karma could be so fickle, and that my future would be far more interesting than I'd imagined.

Chapter 14

The months leading up to Freda's departure passed quickly and quietly. Freda and Fairy had once again become close and were in competition to be the haughtiest. The nasty jabs, pinches and meannesses were replaced by snobbery, cold reserve and talk of high fashion, much of it in the parlor. I could not have cared less, happy to avoid one more uncomfortable situation. Fern and Felicity and I were enjoying the peace that the vacuum of the inn's elite provided us.

Without the help of the other girls the work seemed almost lighter. We would laugh and chat about things at school, such as the goat one of the boys had brought in and let loose in the classroom, and how no one could catch it and all the kids spent too much time trying to corner it and how exasperated the teacher was over the goat and the lost lesson.

Sometimes we talked about the patrons in the taproom, which was just off the front entryway, where the old post office had been before it moved up the street. Father kept it as the taproom because it had easy entrance from the street. He was usually the only one allowed in there with the patrons. Mostly the men sat around and played checkers and smoked cigars and drank a little beer, but once in a while they would get a bit loud, and at these times we liked to stand outside in the entryway and listen, sometimes peeking in to see who was causing the ruckus. Father didn't open it every day, usually only on payday and the day after so the guests wouldn't be disturbed by the comings and goings of millworkers. But when a guest wanted a beer or a drink Father was very willing to open it and sit down for a visit.

The inn was often busy with guests, most of whom caused little trouble, but on occasion some might get rowdy. One day a couple was signing in at the front desk and Mother, who was usually there to register people, recognized the young man. She asked if they were married and he said yes and both of them nodded, but the girl seemed nervous and timid. Mother proceeded to ask more questions: Where do you work? Haven't I seen you down at the beach with another girl? That question and several others were catching the fellow off guard and causing the girl to shrink further and further back towards the door, carpetbag in hand, until finally she backed out and was seen walking swiftly up the sidewalk. When the door closed the man looked back at it, then at Mother, cussed and told her to forget it, then turned and went out after the girl. Mother told us how she had saved the virtue of another young lady and how we should always protect our virtue and not be the simple dupe of our desires.

Another marital intervention occurred when a couple was heard raising their voices and then quieting down, then raising their voices again. Finally Father, seeking to calm them, invited the man to the taproom, where the two sat smoking cigars over a couple of beers. From what we could hear through the door, the man was having difficulties with his wife's refusal to obey him and he was determined to have his way. He thanked my father for the help, saying he'd locked her in the room and expected her to be more compliant when he returned. When he did he found his wallet gone and the bedsheets tied together and thrown out the open window, allowing his acrobatic spouse to escape. He ran outside hollering that if he caught her she would be sorry, peering up the road and then down, but the disobedient wife was nowhere to be seen. Father brought him back to the taproom and they talked until quite late. Afterward Father tumbled up the stairs, grateful he said for such a compliant wife. Florence corrected him. "Patient, you mean. Patient wife." A snore was the reply.

Of course we had our share of people who became inebriated and vomited in their rooms. That was one of the things I hated, cleaning up vomit, but with bleach, baking soda and rags I tackled the task.

Another time we had a guest maybe thirty years old who said he was here on a hunting trip and carried a long satchel of what he explained were guns. The coachman who brought him from the train stopped back later and talked to Mother. Mother talked to Father and that evening they both ate in the dining room with the guests. Later that evening the sheriff came down and arrested the man and took him to the jail. The coachman told Mother the man was asking about Mr. Allen, at one time a prominent businessman in town, who the man said was a philanderer with whom his wife was cheating on him. During supper the man asked where the mill was and who owned it, saying he was looking for a job there. Since most of our guests were from out of town it was not unusual that no one knew Mr. Allen's whereabouts. My father, aware of the story, prodded the man, asking why he would want to work for someone so disagreeable. The fellow took the bait, Father asked more questions, and little by little, as the other guests left, his story came out. Father, shrewd in many ways, agreed with the man and said he'd heard stories about Mr. Allen's indiscretions. Mother excused herself and told Foster to run to the sheriff and bring him back. When the sheriff arrived Mother explained the whole situation to him and led him to the man's room, where they found several rifles and cartridges and a telescope directed at the roadway where numerous carriages and people traveled every day. The sheriff, convinced this was an unstable character, removed the guns to the inn's office and then went to the dining room to confront the man. Realizing he had been tricked, the man tried to escape. When he couldn't he attacked the sheriff, but of course with Father there to help the man was manacled and taken to the jail. The sheriff said things would be sorted out later.

This was our day-to-day life, working to keep an inn running and occasionally encountering some little excitement that enlivened our existence.

Our next excitement was Freda's going-away supper, which occasioned much more preparation than I thought necessary. We set our table formally with wine and the fancy silver and crystal we were seldom allowed to use. The candelabras were laden with many candles and the table looked formal and stunning. When Freda came down that evening before she left and saw it she displayed rare humility and emotion, even shedding a couple tears and hugging us all, even me. We'd prepared a sumptuous supper and the wine made everyone cheerful and Father told jokes, laughing loudly at each of them.

All this hoopla over Freda overshadowed Felicity's and my birthday, which was the next day. The mood was subdued after Freda's departure and there was only a token celebration for Felicity and me with a little cake and presents from Mother and Father. I was embarrassed by the affair. Felicity was as usual gracious about the small gifts and cake and thanked everyone. My gifts from the family were a new apron and dust hat and a small porcelain dish for my hairpins, for which I too thanked everyone.

I said nothing, but after supper was cleaned up and we were getting ready for bed I told Felicity I had a surprise birthday present for her. She was embarrassed, saying she had not gotten me anything. I hushed her, had her sit down and close her eyes, and put the simply-wrapped present into her hands. She squeezed it and poked it but could not guess the contents. When I said she could open her eyes she unwrapped the present, the pin cushion and the packet of needles and the little velveteen pouch. Peering into the pouch she drew in her breath quickly and dumped the little silver thimble out onto her hand. It was beautifully worked and indeed a rare treasure. She looked at me seriously.

"Where did you get this?"

"At the store. That's what I was working for."

"You bought it for me?" She was incredulous. Why would anyone buy her such an elegant gift? Who would care so much about the little mouse who felt she was of no consequence?

"Yes, for you." She put it on her finger and it fit perfectly. She came over to me and hugged me as hard as I imagined she could, then again kissed me lightly on the lips.

Any thought of a schism was dashed. We were as close as ever.

But the kiss stirred something indefinable in me, an excitement I had never felt before. I could still feel her lips long after. My sister. My dear, dear sister.

Chapter 15

That next year went both quickly and slowly. We were busy with the inn, and with Fern spending so much time at the factory learning bookkeeping I had to work harder than ever. I was grateful to be getting a small salary. I put it into my worn change purse, a hand-me-down from Mother.

I went through my daily routine trying always to streamline every task so I could do it faster and more efficiently and perhaps at the end of the day have a few minutes to sit with everyone or have a cup of tea with Felicity.

I was somewhat grateful when the number of guests in autumn dropped off a little, giving me more free hours, but I found my leisure taken up with other pastimes. Fern had lent me a book in which I became engrossed, and after that I spent more time at the library picking out good novels. Evenings we would sit in our room newly lit by the gas lights Father had had installed. I would read while Felicity mended clothes, her silver thimble glistening in the light. Just as I had imagined, seeing her use the thimble gave me great satisfaction. She would look up and smile as though she had read my mind.

My days without Freda were comfortable, no longer filled with cringing or avoidance and tension and pain. Fairy was not following as closely in Freda's footsteps as Freda would probably have liked. Fairy was still looking forward to attending the new school but she was quieter, gentler.

I was becoming more comfortable in the family, feeling as though I almost was a part of it. Of course no one said anything. They wouldn't, but as the tension relaxed we found we enjoyed being together more. The supper table was full of chatter about our day. Frequently Father would talk a lot because his was the most interesting. He'd tell jokes or talk about the funnier happenings at work and then, as always, laugh louder and longer than anyone else. When Fern and Felicity and I did our evening chores the time went more quickly and even seemed fun. We would joke or sometimes splash a little water on each other. Lately Father had taken to sitting at the cleared kitchen table and reading aloud interesting news articles from the paper. We always enjoyed that and he said it broadened all of our worlds more than stale history classes did. One night he read about an area of London called Whitechapel, where an evil man nicknamed Jack the Ripper was murdering women. He would not give us details except to say the crimes were horrific and the murderer had not been caught. We all listened in morbid fascination. That night Fairy, now sleeping alone, awoke with a nightmare and came into our room. When she tried to climb in with Felicity, a difficult fit, Felicity moved into my bed and snuggled up close under my arm. That was comfortable but somehow caused me to lie awake all night, conscious of this small warm body next to mine.

One night there was a ruckus outside and when I peeked out the window I saw one of the factories on fire. This was terribly frightening. I woke Felicity and we roused the rest of the family and all of us threw on some clothes and walked uptown to see the spectacle. The firemen came with their horses and their pumper cart and sprayed water onto the fire, pumping and pumping, but to no avail. Then they started to spray the nearby factories so they would not catch fire too. The H.W. Kimble Satinet factory was fully engulfed, flames shooting out the windows. It looked as bright as day and was so hot we all had to back away. There must have been two hundred people assembled on the street. I could smell tar and oil and all manner of things in the smoke. We were all watching, mesmerized, when suddenly the roof collapsed, sending a shower of sparks and debris into the air and causing everyone to cry out and back off still more. The firemen led the horses farther away, having wisely unharnessed them from the pumper cart. They were out of water and were trying to run a hose into the brook that ran through the town, using the hand pump to draw water up, but nothing was going to put out that fire. Mr. Kimble finally came down the hill in his buggy, but he too couldn't get close. He had someone hold the reins as he walked up to the fire chief. We could see them talking, Mr. Kimble gesticulating and finally putting his hand to his head. Pulling out a handkerchief he blew his nose. We all felt sorry for him. Imagine seeing your business go up in flames and you are helpless to stop it. Fortunately no one was in the building; that would have made it a hundred times worse. As the flames died down a little and it looked as though no other structure would become involved, Father went up to the firemen and invited them to the inn, hoping to refresh them after such hard work. He told us to go back and brew up some coffee, make tea, and cut cold beef from the roast for sandwiches. We rushed back to get the dining room ready.

It had been chilly outside and you noticed it if you were not close to the fire, so we tucked a couple large logs into the dining room and parlor fireplaces. As people arrived they moved close to the fire and rubbed their hands together, holding them out to the flames, and then turned their backs to it to warm their other side. Some of them seemed to be clothed in only their nightwear with a coat thrown over it.

We had been out watching the fire for several hours and now it was three in the morning, but not only did the firemen come but also half the spectators. The rooms smelled of smoke. The mood was festive, with everyone talking about the incredible scene. When Mr. Kimble arrived Father took him into the taproom and gave him a larger than normal whiskey. The firemen had coffee, then beer, sandwiches, and some leftover cake. Everyone helped themselves. The table was starting to look bare until we went to the pantry and found a half wheel of cheese, some soda crackers, and apples we sliced thin. We thought it enough to sate the hungry horde.

Father was generous. He knew that people needed to come together after tragedies and this helped them while helping him to keep his good standing in the community. Later he said if he ever wanted to run for a local government seat, hosting things like that would stick in people's memory when all the talk of what changes you intended to make had faded.

The next day the grocer's delivery boy came with a larger than usual delivery since our pantry had been reduced considerably. His horse pawed the ground as he unloaded the boxes and I could see him moving slowly, eyeing me.

Finally he spoke. "Fancy a cup of tea? That would taste real good right now."

I was taken aback. No one had ever made even the vaguest overture to me. "Excuse me?"

"You know." Now he was the one taken aback. "Have a cup of tea with me."

"What? I have no time for tea. I work here. I can't dawdle." I was surprised. Not only did I not have time for tea but I didn't want it with him either.

"Well, excuse me." His words were tinged with sarcasm. Tipping his cap he climbed back onto his wagon, and as he turned the horse around it chose that moment to drop a steaming pile of dung. The boy looked back and sneered as the horse clopped down the drive.

I was left standing there, a box of groceries in my arms, wondering what had just happened.

Then I went inside and made tea for Felicity and me.

Chapter 16

The grocery boy shook me up. What was I thinking? I have no future here at the inn, none except drudgery. Why would I react so harshly when he only wanted to be friendly?

As I matured my body was going through more of the changes I had watched all the girls in the family experience. I had seen Freda and Fairy blossom sooner than the rest of us. Fern followed shortly after, but I did not seem to change much. Then, several months after Freda left, I found myself unable to fit into my clothes. Felicity helped, letting seams out as much as possible, and finally I got Fairy's outgrown hand-me-downs, which then had to be taken in. Felicity was kept busy, the little silver thimble flashing in the evening light.

Felicity was filling out more too and I was happy to see she was not as sickly as she once had been.

None of this was lost on Foster.

One morning when I took a basket to the root cellar to collect vegetables for our evening soup Foster was there. He too had grown and was now taller than me, as tall as Fern. He blocked my way out. Thinking he was playing a game I pushed into him, but he held fast. Grabbing the basket away from me he shoved me up against the rock wall and tried to kiss me.

"What are you doing?" I shouted, but of course no one could hear me in the earth-insulated cellar. I pushed him away, shocked at his audacity.

"I love you, Millie. I have always loved you." I stared. I had no knowledge or understanding of his proclamation.

"What do you mean? I'm your sister, silly." At this he thrust the basket back into my arms. Turning about he rushed out the door with a backward shot, "You're not my sister and I love you."

I stood there, dazed, wondering what had just happened. Even though the day was warm, the root cellar with its store of ice sent a chill through me. How did he know our real relationship? Why hadn't I seen this before? Yes, I had noticed he watched me at chores and followed me to the market with an offer to help carry things back to the house, but I had never expected this. Did I just hurt his feelings? Should I have been more careful? But I was so surprised!

As I peeled potatoes and cut up carrots I thought about the morning, playing it back in my mind. Ordinarily Foster would have been sitting at the table watching me do chores, but he wasn't there. Should I have said something to Mother?

At supper that evening Foster was quieter than usual and sat hunched over his plate. Several times Father tried to rouse him but he would only mumble a reply and continue to eat. Once I saw him look at me from below his lowered brow. I smiled at him, trying to let him know I was not angry, but he just looked down again and continued to eat. Before the meal was finished he asked to be excused and left the table. Father and Mother exchanged glances.

"I wonder if Foster is feeling unwell," Mother said after he left. "He didn't say a word at supper, did he?" She looked around the table for confirmation.

We went about our regular cleanup as Father read an article in the paper that said a new invention called an automobile would replace the horse and carriage and in a few years, and the production of hundreds and hundreds of them on a new thing called an assembly line might bring the price down low enough for more common people to purchase them.

Foster did not reappear. Normally he sat at the table distractedly going through the paper Father had finished with.

Once we completed our chores Fern hurriedly excused herself to read a new book she was excited about. She said *The Adventures of Huckleberry Finn* was fun and engrossing, suggesting that Foster should read it when she finished.

Felicity and I were left to amuse ourselves. We sat at the kitchen table, I polishing silver, my seemingly my never-ending chore, and she mending clothes, a button sewn on here, a sock darned there. I tried to think of a way to work Foster into our small talk.

"Hasn't Foster grown," I started.

"Oh yes, and isn't he getting handsome? He will be quite a catch some day." Felicity was always ready with a compliment.

"Do you think he has a sweetheart? Have you ever seen him with a girl at school?" I should know this as well as anyone, but I was casting about for something to help me understand his actions and provide an opening to more conversation.

"I have never heard him speak of anyone. Perhaps he's just too young to think of girls."

"Yes. Perhaps." I didn't know how to tell her.

That evening Felicity went upstairs before me and on my way up the back staircase Foster met me coming down. He stood in front of me. I stopped.

"I'm sorry. Don't hate me. I can't help myself." His tone was weak and pleading.

"I don't hate you, Foster. You're my brother. I love you. But I love you as a brother."

In a second his face and voice changed. "Humph. You love me as a brother? But how do you love Felicity?" Now his tone was malicious and taunting.

"What?" Again Foster had truly shocked me. This was not the naïve boy of our youth.

He turned and went back up the stairs, leaving me dazed and thinking of Felicity's kiss in the root cellar, remembering the warmth of that day and the chill of the ice.

Chapter 17

Felicity was already asleep by the time I was ready for bed. I looked at her face, soft and peaceful in the lamplight. Was Foster revealing to me feelings I had repressed? If it was obvious to him did others see it? How did I feel about Felicity? Certainly I loved her as a sister. Everyone loved her. Who would not love such a sweet and guileless child? But she wasn't a child anymore. She was a woman. A lovely gentle woman. And I was, she said, her dear sister.

I was not in love with her. I knew that would be wrong. I knew I should be looking to the grocer boy, to Foster, to one of the workers in Father's factory or even to one of the upper-crust family boys if he would have me.

I could not tell anyone what had happened with Foster. I would be very nice to him. I did not have any unnatural feelings for Felicity. I would encourage the grocery boy. My mind was a swirl and I fell asleep tormented over these new happenings in my life.

The next morning I rose and dressed and went to the kitchen to do my chores long before the rest of the family. Percolating the coffee, making biscuits, slicing bacon, putting linens in to soak, I busied myself while trying to find just the right treat to appeal to Foster. I planned to go to the market later and along with a few other purchases buy a bottle of Coca-Cola syrup, which was becoming a favorite in the house.

Father was being more careful about whom he served in the taproom and when. He'd read about a group of women opposed to drinking who were trying to outlaw it and had even succeeded in Kansas. The Women's Christian Temperance Union was out to shut down all saloons and Father hoped if he was discreet he might be ignored. After a while he asked his "regular guests" to enter through the rear of the inn. To the consternation of some, he insisted they not go home inebriated nor stay so late their wives were forced to come after them. He started to bring in other beverages and one of the favorites was Coca-Cola, which he mixed with seltzer and served to the ladies in the dining room and to Foster, who favored it over all other beverages.

Another favorite of Foster's was deviled eggs so I started a large kettle of water boiling with eggs that I could devil later while preparing supper.

Everyone thought I was babying Foster because he seemed under the weather, but Foster knew.

I had tea with the grocer boy. I brought Father dinner and walked through the factory to deliver it and see if any of the boys caught my fancy and I caught their eye. Indeed a number of heads turned and Father said I should consider not delivering his dinner in the future because too many of the boys got distracted.

That night Father offered to have a picnic for his factory workers, understanding I'm sure that I needed to meet a nice boy. "Circulate" was what he said to Mother; "Millie needs to circulate." Foster sat across the table with a wry smile, sure of his knowledge that in the end I wouldn't be taken with any of them. But he said nothing and just continued smiling. I had no idea when he had become so vindictive. Some of Freda must have rubbed off onto him.

Father said he couldn't have a picnic this late in the year since it was too cold out but next year he would be sure to have a special one.

Fall was over and winter upon us. Trips to the market were through snow and ice. We were grateful to be so close to the market, the church and the library.

Freda came home for the Christmas holiday. She was thinner and even more confident if that was possible. She showed off her new manners and didn't bother to tease or make fun of me, instead ignoring me as though I were invisible. Freda, Fairy and Foster kept busy making the rounds of the neighbors bringing little cakes and glorying in the fuss made over them. I stayed home to make the little cakes and the cookies that enlivened the season and made the inn smell like heaven.

Mother took Fern and Felicity on a shopping trip to Willimantic, leaving me home with the excuse that someone must be there to take care of Freda and her consorts when they came in from one of their visits. But, Mother assured me, they would find some finery for me on the trip.

Our Christmas dinner was gayer than ever. We walked across the street to the church, our way illuminated by moonlight. Candles in the windows promised warmth within. We could hear horses clomping and sleigh bells jingling as they came closer, passed us and drove further down the road. The church was filled with people, and the candles we could see from the road flickered even more richly inside. An overwhelming sense of wellbeing filled me, and for a few minutes I lost myself in song and prayer and my troubles melted away. I left early to go back and set up a midnight buffet with warm punch, cold meats and spiced pies. Everyone returned and there was much merriment. Mother even sat down to the piano and pounded out a few tunes, and one of our boarders followed with a ragtime. We danced and ate, sang and laughed until the clock struck three and everyone collapsed while Fern and I cleaned up a little. Foster had passed out on the settee from too much punch and then slid down onto the rug. I covered him with a quilt and tucked a little pillow under his head. He looked so much like an angel that I gave him a kiss on the cheek. I wondered if in the morning he would remember it and think he was dreaming.

Freda went back to school shortly after New Year's Day and was comfortably ensconced when the blizzard hit. It snowed and blew starting on Sunday and didn't stop for three days. The temperature went from fifty degrees to well below zero. The winds were paralyzing. Several shutters in need of repair banged rhythmically until Father, clothed head to toe in fur, went out and nailed them shut, saying he'd fix them when the weather cleared. Not only did we have our regular boarders but several nearby families came in for over a week when they had run out of coal and were not able to keep warm. Fortunately the people who were arriving came before the worst of the storm hit and even then they had to crawl through thigh-high snow and sometimes waist-high drifts.

When the storm finally let up some parts of the house had snowdrifts up to the second-story windows, but around other parts of the house the ground was almost scoured bare from the wind. Fortunately the door was in one of the bare spots, allowing us to carry in wood for the fireplaces. Father stoked the furnace with coal and we were as comfortable as we could be. The pantry was full enough and Foster dug a path to the root cellar through the waist-high snow. On the edges of the path the snow was piled up to his shoulders.

When Father was able to walk to the post office he found a letter from Freda saying she was safe and concerned about us. He wrote back to her immediately and told her how high the snow was and how we were doing.

I shall never forget that snow. I've never since seen such a storm and hope never to again.

Chapter 18

In the late spring Freda was due home after her first year away at school. A ball was planned in honor of her return. The fourth-floor ballroom was cleaned and readied. We hadn't used it in several years and some areas seemed in disrepair. Father brought in a team of workers from the factory to spruce it up. The boys moved the chairs out, cleaned, painted and polished the floor, then moved the chairs back to the room's perimeter and placed tables for serving drinks and hors d'oeuvres. Father had the dramatic heavy drapes cleaned so they looked like new.

Printed invitations went out to all the prominent families in town and to the local politicians and clergy. No one was left out and most replied saying they would join us. Men Father met in passing talked about how excited their wives and daughters were. The town was in a tizzy of anticipation.

When Freda arrived she was welcomed with fanfare. Father and Mother met her at the station in a rented coach. She must have felt like a princess. The rest of us waited on the back lawn to greet her and gave out a hurrah when she arrived. As she stepped out of the coach I could see a difference. Was she more polished, more poised and more congenial? Dressed in a feminine riding habit with top hat and veil in the back, ankle-length skirt and boots, she did look the very picture of a magazine cover. I couldn't believe it– she was actually speaking to everyone! Kindly! Even to me! I was mesmerized by the change, but as I studied her movements while she greeted the family I could still see the serpent coiled below the surface, only now that surface was smooth as a mirror and the serpent was held tightly in check.

Our parents settled Freda into a separate guestroom. No longer was she the girl packed with her sister into one bedroom. At supper she held a place of honor and Mother and Fairy flanked her with Father at the other end. I doubt she was so favored at her boarding school, but without anyone to tell us differently we had to believe that she was indeed a good student and well-liked. The first crack in her façade came when she complained that her wardrobe was too plebeian, at which Mother drew in her breath sharply but did not utter a word. She talked about the other girls who lived close by the school and her visits to their "magnificent" homes. Their fathers were doctors and lawyers and politicians, and she was careful not to add that they were not factory managers or innkeepers. She spoke of crystal chandeliers and silk dresses, of gigantic Persian carpets and bone china. She talked and talked of the excesses, but said little of how she liked the school, the teachers or her classmates. I sat there wondering if anyone else was feeling mortified by the time and expense that had gone into the ball, which, no matter how grand, could never measure up to her high standard.

We sat, listened, and asked questions, all of which she answered with her chin up and head flicking this way and that so that her curls sprang and landed just so when the haughty head settled. I almost peed my pants when I caught Fairy gazing at her and drooling. I jabbed Fern in the ribs and we both had to stifle a giggle, which turned a couple of heads towards us for a moment. But not for long could the family keep their eyes off this now-sophisticated woman in our midst.

After supper she went into the parlor with Mother and Father. Father was no longer content to sit at the table and read us the paper. Foster and Fairy joined them after performing a few trivial chores. Fern, Felicity and I did our usual evening tasks knowing that in a few days we would be back to normal, or so we hoped.

The next day Mother took Freda to Hartford. No longer would the Willimantic shops do for Freda. While they were gone the rest of us continued preparations for the ball. The girls were getting excited, trying on their dresses and making changes and finally deciding that no more could be done. The food was ordered; Father saw to it that on this occasion I would neither prepare nor serve. A small orchestra arrived the day before and set up in the ballroom and rehearsed that evening. They shared several rooms and ate supper with our boarders and treated them to a couple of songs.

Mother and Freda arrived late, telling us the train had been delayed in Manchester. They had a late supper together which Fairy and Foster attended, ostensibly to keep them company.

Everyone was keyed up over the ball, even Freda, although she made a great pretense of casualness about it.

Chapter 19

Most of us woke early the morning of the ball. But not Freda. Even if she didn't arrive early for breakfast we knew she was awake because Fairy was reporting on her every move. We sent Fairy back up with coffee and toast to ensure the royal one wouldn't starve.

Father had ordered a pair of fine gold earrings for her from a jeweler in Willimantic. He showed them off at breakfast before she came down.

I could not understand the mammoth magnitude of the attention that was being lavished upon Freda. Would each of us get this in our turn? The time and expense were daunting. Could we afford this? Father must know best. I could only imagine what celebrations the family would face when Foster left the nest. But as usual I said nothing and only Fern felt as I did, wondering what the huge fuss was about. We thought there might be more to it and that perhaps we might find out at the ball.

Trays and trays of treats went into the root cellar, where a boy with a lantern and a broom kept guard and frightened away mice. When I went in to get a corned beef for our simple lunch I frightened the dickens out of the boy, who jumped and almost knocked a tray over. They were sitting atop several large blocks of ice that had been dusted with sawdust and then covered in burlap, their slow melting moistening the burlap and cooling even more that corner of the cellar.

I was enjoying one of the easiest days of my life. With other people to cook, I served only a simple meal of corned beef on the baker's rye bread with dill pickles. No pots, no pans, just a few more plates and napkins than usual. I was hoping Father would take pity on me after the ball and have someone help with the cleanup too.

I was a woman of leisure and sat at the kitchen table with a coffee and one of the magazines Freda had brought home with her. It felt odd to watch the busyness around me. It was like being in the center of the hurricane, watching the chaos but remaining untouched. I was usually part of the chaos, the organizer of the chaos. How dull it would be to have a life of leisure, sitting and drinking coffee and reading magazines.

I was absently thinking this when Freda came pounding down the stairs, all worked up and far from the poised damsel from the previous evening.

"Where's my valise? Did you see it? It's missing and I can't find it." She had an urgent frustrated tone.

I looked blankly at her.

"Didn't you hear me? My valise! Did you see it?"

"Your valise?" I didn't immediately understand.

"My valise, you moron! My bag!" She was in perfect Freda form. I shook my head. "I don't know."

"And have you seen Felicity? She was supposed to fix the hem on my gown! Where is she?"

I shrugged my shoulders.

"What good are you?" She uttered this like a curse and thumped back up the stairs. I could hear her calling Felicity. I mused about following her to make sure she wasn't mean to my sister, but instead I just sat as though in a trance. I had never had time to think about my life. I was always too busy planning the meal, cooking the meal, serving the meal, cleaning up after the meal, washing the linens, washing the clothes, ordering the food—the list went on and on and on. Here I was sitting at the table on the busiest day the inn had ever seen, and I had nothing to do. It was the strangest feeling, having time to ponder my life.

Foster came in.

"Have you seen my grey cravat? I thought I put it in the laundry to be freshened last week."

I gazed at him, shaking my head, feeling out of my realm.

"No, I don't remember seeing it."

"You know, the grey one?"

"No, I don't remember it."

He too stormed out.

Soon Fairy arrived. She looked at me, opened her mouth, thought better of it, then turned and went back up the stairs.

I started to laugh. I almost fell off the chair laughing. When Fern and Felicity came down they sat at the table with me and gave me puzzled looks but then they too started to laugh with me. Mother came in and stood silently, and shortly our laughter quieted down.

"You girls are acting so silly when everyone is trying to get ready. Why are you being so idiotic?"

This hurt. Mother almost never said mean things. She seemed very annoyed. We sobered up.

"Sorry. What can we do to help?" Felicity spoke up for us all.

"Well, first of all, Felicity, Freda needs some help with her hem. Fern, Millie, why don't you try to find Freda's valise." We all rose to move on. I was grateful to have something to focus on other than my ridiculous life.

Chapter 20

Again I had received one of Fairy's hand-me-downs, but it was much finer than my Sunday best and Felicity helped me spruce it up with lace and ribbon and some extra flounces that were in style. I felt as though I made a fairly good presentation in it.

Fern had a bustle and big bow on the back to make her flatter bottom more pronounced. Fairy was lovely with a bustle and lots of fabric draped in the front. Felicity was of course always beautiful and arrived in an elegantly understated gown.

Foster was handsome in his black bow tie and tails, having apparently rethought the cravat. Freda was stunning, her tight corset pushing her ivory breasts up and almost out of her sleeveless satin dress with a hobble-skirt that she managed to swish around in dramatically. Her hair was piled in a cluster of ringlets that Mother must have helped her arrange. Long white gloves finished off the effect.

Several of the supervisors from Father's factory ushered guests from the front door to the fourth-floor landing. Thus the transition from the street to the ballroom went smoothly.

We stood on the landing at the top of the stairs, just outside the ballroom, greeting our guests as they arrived. One of us girls took the arm of single men and Foster took the arm of any lady without an escort or accompanying her parents. Mother and Father stayed near the entryway until most guests had arrived. All were ushered into the ballroom and introduced to others, then released to their new acquaintances. Mother had schooled us all on the proper etiquette for every step of the evening, and so far it was going perfectly.

When a particularly interesting family arrived that Father thought Freda should be paying special attention to, he would signal her and whisper their names so she could greet them properly. She was then to accompany the family in, but not by herself. That would be too obvious. She and Fairy together would walk them back to the refreshment tables and offer them punch, make a little small talk and then return to the entrance to await the next victims.

The orchestra was instructed to play quiet background music until given the signal from Father, who would decide when the most important people had arrived and the formal welcome and dancing could commence.

When the Kingsburys arrived Father nodded to Freda, who already knew them all and who with Fairy walked them back to the refreshment tables. After punch was offered, introductions made to several others nearby, and small talk exchanged, Freda and Fairy returned. The mayor arrived with his wife but no children. Father gave no signal. The judge with his wife, two daughters and son appeared; Father signaled. The sheriff came with his wife and daughter, and the preacher with his wife, three daughters and two sons. No signal. The Masons arrived with their two sons and Father almost somersaulted. Freda and Fairy dutifully ushered them in. The dry goods merchant arrived with his family. Teachers, butchers and even machinists streamed in, for my benefit I surmised. One of the Cheneys of

Manchester occasioned a twist of Father's moustache, as did some of the mill owners and managers, depending upon their potential earnings. Father was very shrewd in projecting how far a man would go in the world and wasn't leaving Freda's future to chance or romantic whimsy.

Once the quota of sheep had entered the paddock, Father quieted the orchestra and addressed the flock.

"Welcome to our ball, ladies and gentlemen. This evening is to celebrate the close of our Freda's first year"–he turned and motioned to Freda–"at the Farmington School for Young Ladies. We are so very proud of her. Please join us in this celebration and take a few moments to speak to her and ask her for a dance." Father backed away and gently moved Freda forward.

Freda, having never been the shy one, surprised those of us who knew her by fluttering her fan demurely and pausing to offer, "Thank you all for coming to our little ball. I hope you enjoy yourselves and I hope I get the opportunity to dance with each and every one of you." Her gaze rested on several of the most eligible fellows in the crowd.

Father motioned to the orchestra and they struck up a lively tune. While a good number of people shuffled over to the punchbowl, several couples moved to the center of the room and christened our newly polished dance floor.

Fern and I watched from the sidelines as boys shyly slunk through the groups to edge closer to Freda, who was talking smoothly to the mayor. She was glowing. What a transformation from the frazzled puffed-up twit of yesterday.

Fairy flanked her, trying silently to convey to the younger eligibles that she would be available in a couple of years.

As the punchbowl was drained and refilled several times people relaxed and the dance floor filled. Only a few of the older set collected in the chairs or in little groups watching the dancers swing by.

A tall thin serious-looking boy asked Fern to dance and left me looking into my punch. After he deposited Fern back with me her mathematics teacher came up, bowed and requested a dance. I glanced at Father, whose watchful look betrayed concern. Fern, however, was thrilled.

Felicity was never without a partner, all plying her with punch and bringing her back to the family group, from which she always searched for me with her eyes and smiled when she found me.

Fairy danced with several of the younger set and even invited the elder gentlemen of the more prominent families to the floor.

Father and Mother spun around the room several times and then took a rest to visit with their guests, going smoothly from one knot to the next and greeting them all graciously.

Foster had forgotten me, surrounded by sweet girls and admiring young ladies. He was almost overcome with attention and handling it all with smiles and jokes and even at one point trying to dance with three girls at once.

Freda's evening was a success. She was paired with two of the up-and-coming young men in the area. Both seemed pleased with themselves and a friendly competition was developing.

Fern continued to dance with her teacher, at which Father's brow grew more and more furrowed.

The gas lights were lit and the ball went on, punch flowing freely and laughter and chatter almost drowning out the orchestra. The dance floor filled and emptied depending upon the tempo of the music.

A jumble of people floated in eddies and in a smooth motion circled Fern and her teacher, who seemed to be at the center of the human hurricane. Father and Mother stood at the sidelines alternately watching them and turning back, heads bent in discussion, but still pausing to smile and chat with guests who stopped to speak to them.

A machinist from the cartridge factory asked me to dance. I had noticed him upon his arrival and he had caught my eye several times throughout the evening, at first looking away and later smiling shyly. He danced with an awkward confidence that was neither arrogant nor retiring. In a straightforward manner he asked if we could dance again and I said yes. He was of average height and build and had an engaging smile, blue eyes and a fine head of thick curly brown hair. Clean-shaven, dressed neatly in a suit that seemed a tiny bit too small, he walked and moved in a manner that bespoke a more refined upbringing than his attire might imply. We danced several more times and before the end of the evening he asked if he could see me again. I agreed.

I had been watching Father and Mother as they in turn watched their children. For each one of us their focus and their pleasure or concern was obvious to me although the guests would not likely have noticed. They were very satisfied with Freda, Fairy and Foster. They were worked up over Fern and her teacher. I caught Father glancing at me and my partner and looking pleased. They barely glanced at Felicity, who was always surrounded by a throng but who often searched me out.

The crowd gradually thinned. Near midnight people thanked our parents and left. By one o'clock the orchestra had packed up and retired. Father's hires were putting chairs and tables away and carrying the food and dishes to the kitchen.

As Father gathered us all together we were flagging, and in the case of Foster and Felicity, who had both overindulged at the punchbowl, almost unable to stand. Praising us all, he said we would be cleaning up tomorrow. He sent me to help Felicity to bed while he held Fern behind.

Chapter 21

Felicity steadied herself on the banister as she and I stumbled down the stairs to our room on the second floor. I undressed and got into bed. Felicity moved slowly, holding onto the chair as she stood and swayed, occasionally sitting. While I had had enough punch to relax me I had not overindulged.

"Do you feel okay? Do you want me to get you a cup of tea?" I sensed she didn't feel well.

"No, I think I'll be okay, but I can't find my nightdress." I got up, found her chemise and helped her slip it over her head. She hugged me and I felt us both swaying. I was afraid I would fall over but managed to lean against my bed and climb back into it as she sat on hers. I could see her sitting in the dim light, looking at me.

"Did you have a good time tonight? You were always surrounded by the boys." I was curious but also trying to gauge her sobriety, hoping she wouldn't get sick.

"Yes. Did you? It seems you have an admirer." Felicity's slurred words had a most curious tone.

She blew out the candle and climbed in with me.

"You're in the wrong bed." I must have sounded distressed.

"Yes, silly, I am."

She rolled into me, and kissed me full on the mouth, then on my neck, then slipped her hand under my chemise. I couldn't stop her. I didn't want to stop her.

The next morning I was the first in the kitchen. I fed the stove some coal and filled the large kettle for hot water to tackle the huge pile of dishes. I started the coffee and ran out to the chickens to collect the eggs. The pantry held the remains of the ball including a good pile of bread that would be enough for toast. Slicing off a couple pounds of bacon I put it in the large skillet and while it sputtered I cracked and beat a dozen and a half eggs.

Fern appeared. Taking in the state of the kitchen, she poured the hot water into the sink, grated in some soap and attacked the stacks of dishes.

"Fern, you were dancing with Mr. Jenkins quite a lot. Did you have fun?"

"Yes, I had a lot of fun, but Father took me aside last night and told me not to ever embarrass him again. He thinks I should have been dancing with the younger more eligible fellows and not spending my whole evening with Harold."

"Harold? You call him Harold?" I looked up from the eggs to try to see her face. I noted her blush as she turned from the sink to glance at me.

"He said I should." And she went back to washing. After my evening, I was too confused to be shocked.

"Really?" Was all I could muster as I replayed the previous night in my mind.

"And you seemed to have an admirer." Fern had turned to look at me. I must have blushed, but not for the reason she assumed. The night with Felicity was swirling through my head. Then I remembered Johnny.

"Oh, yes, Johnny Knight. He's a very nice boy."

"Knight? And is he your knight in shining armor?" Fern was giggling now.

"Well, he's quite likable and he wants to see me again, so yes, he may be my knight." I didn't know what to say. I'd never been in love. I didn't know what it was supposed to be like. But I knew that what I was feeling for Felicity was the closest I had ever come to it.

Fairy came down the stairs.

"Is the coffee ready? Freda asked to have some before she comes down."

I motioned to the pot and Fairy filled a small pot from it and got a tray and cup.

"I had a wonderful time last night. Did you enjoy it?"

"Yes," Fern answered for us both, "we did. Who did you dance with?" Both Fern and I knew this would lead to mindless chatter about all the people she spoke to and who danced with her and who Freda danced with and any other gossip that might fill her head.

I went out to the dining room to set up coffee and cream and found several guests already waiting. I returned to the kitchen and portioned out breakfast to serve them.

Father and Mother appeared and our morning began. As the family arrived the chatter at the table grew. Everyone had a story about someone, and laughter and good-natured teasing enlivened our morning table.

Apparently Freda had found several suitors who would, as Father put it, "make his princess a very smart match." Freda looked pleased with herself and was more pleasant than usual.

Fairy, sitting next to Freda, was basking in the glow of her oldest sister. Fern caught my eye and her expression of gagging tickled me, but I knew I shouldn't respond to it out loud or I would be chastised for being jealous of Freda's good fortune.

Felicity arrived and Father and Mother spoke of her as the bright light to which all the fellows were attracted. She smiled but looked to me. "But what of Millie? Surely she found her sweetheart last night."

Everyone agreed and I found myself blushing again. They laughed. I focused on buttering my toast, not meeting their eyes for fear I might somehow reveal myself.

There was no mention of Fern, not a single word. That deliberate oversight I am sure pained Fern, who had likely had one of the most enjoyable evenings of her life.

I could hear more guests in the dining room and was glad their needs would occupy me away from the family and any focus on me. As I made up plates to deliver I glanced at Felicity, who was glowing and had never looked happier. I served and collected dishes and kept busy while everyone lingered around the table.

Fern rose to bring her plate to the sink. Still there was not a word to her or about her. I filled the kettle and put it on the stove for more hot water, and since no one was making a motion to leave I made more coffee. Fern helped me at the sink.

A knock at the door brought several of the boys who had danced with Fairy and they asked if she could go to the lake with them, inviting Felicity to join them. Fairy begged to go saying she would help with chores later. Felicity felt she couldn't and perhaps Fern or Freda might want to.

Father hemmed and hawed until Freda, not really wanting to spend her day with the younger set, said she would join them but they must be back for afternoon tea. All agreed and Fairy rushed upstairs to change while Freda, not so excited at being part of the fray, went up more slowly and came down half an hour later. Fairy was dancing around outside, too excited to sit quietly and be a lady, but Freda's stern gaze calmed her. Both could be seen in their broad hats and parasols in hand walking up the sidewalk towards the lake, the boys trailing proudly behind.

Mother watched them from the door.

"My girls are growing up," was all she said before turning back and heading to the laundry room.

Fern and I were busy with the breakfast dishes.

"They didn't say a word about me." She sounded hurt. "Not a word."

"Don't worry. They love you. They just want what's best for you." I was trying to comfort her.

"But how would they know what's best for me? I am not like the rest of them. They don't know me, and they don't understand me." I couldn't disagree.

Chapter 22

The next evening I heard Fern slip down the back stairs. I knew her footfall as we all know our family's steps. When I went to the window the moonlight illuminated her running across the lawn into the arms of Mr. Jenkins. I wouldn't tell. I was happy for her and hoped our parents would see their way to accepting the alliance.

I climbed back into my bed next to Felicity, who hadn't left my side since the night of the ball. Her caresses were what I yearned for the whole day as I forced myself to pretend that a casual brush of her hand at supper didn't raise my ardor.

The summer passed quickly, full of frequent comings and goings. Fairy was constantly going out, to the store for an ice cream, to the lake, for "just a walk." Freda had guests in the parlor, and on those occasions Father once again sat at the kitchen table reading the paper to the rest of us.

He was worried, he said, because a Philadelphia rail line was in financial trouble and he thought it might cause panic if it failed. He had just taken a large quantity of his funds and put it into gold in an effort, he said, to protect the inn and our future. In my ignorance I couldn't understand why a Pennsylvania railroad would affect us, but Father was very shrewd and had planned wisely. Still, we were all told to be more careful in planning how we spent money for the inn. He said he was glad Freda's last year in Farmington was already paid for and told Fairy she might have to wait an extra year before she could go.

When Freda wasn't entertaining her guests she was holed up in her room fussing with her hair or working on her wardrobe. Mother often sat with her for hours grooming her for high society. I could not understand how anyone could be satisfied spending their time so idly.

Fern quietly went about her life and chores, still willing to help around the inn. I was grateful for so diligent a sister. Father and Mother never again mentioned her night at the ball and hoped that time would fix what they could not. But I knew her secret and one evening when we were alone doing the dishes I told her so. I reassured her, saying I was happy for her and I would tell no one. She seemed relieved and even happy to have a confidant. She said she was in love and very happy except that our parents were so set against it. I asked her what she was going to do and she replied she didn't yet know. Then she asked about me. She said she knew. I paused, taken aback.

"What do you mean?" I tried to sound innocent.

"Don't be afraid. I don't think anyone else has a clue. You know, about Felicity." I was shocked. Frightened and shocked and ashamed.

"I don't know what to do. I don't how or why it happened. It just did, and now we can't stop." I sat down at the table and started to cry, wiping my eyes with the dishtowel I had in my hand.

Fern hugged me, trying to comfort me.

"Don't feel bad. You care for each other don't you? Don't be embarrassed. We can't choose these things, I know that better than anyone. It's not as bad as it might seem."

"But she's my sister. My–my–sister!" I tripped on the words.

"Shhhh. Don't fret. It's okay. She's not your sister by blood." She patted me. "I'm going to brew us up some tea." And as she went about the mundane task of brewing tea I did calm down, at least on the surface.

"If you know about us, who else does?" I asked nervously.

"I don't think anyone else pays attention, to either you or me. We're safe." She sounded both resigned and confident. As we drank Felicity arrived with her basket of mending, spread pieces of it out on the table and poured herself some of the tea.

"May I join you?" We both smiled at her. She pulled out her sewing needles and darning egg, retrieved her silver thimble, polished it on her sleeve and went to work, looking contentedly from one of us to the other. At her glance a warm flush and rush of joy filled me.

The next evening after supper Father was at the table, along with everyone else except Freda, who was again in the parlor with the suitor who was her favorite today.

Father opened the paper and read about what they called the gold rush in the Klondike of Alaska. Apparently someone had discovered gold and a number of people were going there to get in on the strike. Foster asked a lot of questions and when Father was done with the paper he read the article and sat for a long time reading and re-reading it.

Fairy left to join Mother and Freda in the parlor. She said she was going to the library with a fellow she'd been spending time with whom Father didn't like. Apparently he was a worker in one of the mills and Father didn't want her associating with someone of, he said, that level. The rest of us could not see the harm in it, but he thought it would dampen the interests of the more affluent families.

I had continued to spend time with Johnny, who understood that my many responsibilities at the inn didn't leave me a lot of time to gad about. He'd come several times a week to sit and have tea or sometimes walk me to the store for an ice cream. He'd drink his tea with a large slice of my pie, which he devoured appreciatively.

I liked Johnny but I was confused by the conflicting feelings I had. My inner turmoil only Fern understood. Felicity, it would seem, had no such conflict. She knew what she felt and what she wanted.

All of these adventures came to a surprising finale one fine August day.

Chapter 23

When Father came home from work and we sat down to supper Foster wasn't among us. After ten minutes I was sent up to his room to remind him what time it was.

When I opened the door I knew something was amiss. Clothes were strewn about the room and his coat was missing. Then I noticed on his dresser an envelope addressed to Mother and Father. I brought it down to the dining room. Everyone had already started eating when I handed the envelope to Father, who looked at me questioningly.

"Foster is not in his room and this was on his dresser."

Father ripped it open and began to read.

He jumped up, almost knocking the table over.

"He's gone, Flo!" he exclaimed. "He's gone to Alaska!" He sat back down with a thump as Mother rushed over to take the letter and read it herself.

"This is insane. What would possess him to run off like this?" Father was shaking.

Mother rushed up the stairs and in a few minutes came back down crying.

"He's gone and he's taken the gold watch we gave him on his thirteenth birthday and some cash that I knew he had in his treasure box. Fitzy, he's gone!"

"I'm going to the sheriff." Father was quick to act. "I'll see if they can find him or stop the train or something." And he grabbed his hat and rushed out the door.

Mother sat back down at the table and stared blankly ahead, not eating, not speaking.

I got up and put on a pot of tea. Fern went into the taproom for a bottle of brandy and poured a small glass.

"Here." She handed it to Mother. "Drink this." And Mother did.

We were all in shock. Fern went to the stack of newspapers that we saved and pulled out the one with the article about the gold rush, but the article was gone. Foster had taken it.

Father came back about two hours later with the sheriff and they both went up to Foster's room for about half an hour. Then the sheriff spoke to Mother for a few minutes and left looking very concerned.

Father saw the brandy and poured himself a small glass and some more for Mother.

"They are going to look for him. They are telegraphing Hartford and Springfield to see if they can find him on the train. They will do everything they can." He sat down at the table and held Mother's hand as they looked blankly at each other. Obviously their thoughts were miles away. We bustled about the kitchen cleaning up.

That evening I heard Fern slipping out again. I got up to look out the window and saw Harold at the edge of the maple's moon-darkened shadow. Fern ran out and handed him something and they both rushed out to the sidewalk. I had a bad feeling about this. What if Fern were running off with Harold?

The next morning Fern did not come down to join me while I did the morning chores. I was afraid to go upstairs and find another letter so I went about my usual ritual, hoping someone would soon come who might wonder where Fern was and go up to her room and look.

Felicity came down and poured herself a small pot of tea. Sitting at the table with her inevitable basket of mending she watched me take the hot bread out of the oven and start to scramble the eggs. When I glanced at her, mending in hand and little thimble on her finger and smiling the most contented and glowing smile as she held my gaze, I experienced another one of those moments that will be forever pressed into my memory. That picture of contentment and love would carry me through the days and months and years that followed.

"Where is Fern?" Felicity was the first to notice.

"I don't know. She hasn't come down yet."

Fairy arrived, sat down and asked for coffee, which I served her. Then she asked when the eggs and bacon would be ready and I answered they would be finished soon and offered her some warm bread and butter, which she devoured as though famished.

"Where is Fern?" Fairy too noticed Fern's absence but was looking around as though more interested in why breakfast wasn't further along.

"She hasn't come down yet," Felicity answered.

Mother was next. When she arrived she helped, slicing more bread and checking for guests in the dining room, which was empty so far. She poured a carafe of coffee to keep warm on the back of the stove, ready to serve to the guests later.

"Where's Fern?" Mother seemed actually concerned. "She is always down by now." She wiped her hands on her apron and ascended the back stairs to rouse Fern.

We could hear her scream from the kitchen.

"Oh heavens!" was the harshest curse she could muster as she ran down the hall to the room she shared with Father. We heard a shout but couldn't determine from where. It was about twenty minutes before both of them appeared, Mother's eyes red, Father with only suspenders, no vest, hair barely combed, moustache drooping, letter in hand. Both of them dropped down into chairs at the kitchen table.

"Fern is gone." Father was the first to speak. "You may as well know that she has run off with that bugger Jenkins. I should call the sheriff, but she is old enough and I wouldn't have the legal rights." We all sat down at the table and listened as Father continued. "What an evil character, preying on my daughter like that. He knew she was too bright and vulnerable and would fall prey to an educated mind like his. He took advantage of her!" Father slammed his hand down hard on the table and we all jumped.

"Did any of you know about this?" He looked around the table and all of us shook our heads. "Well, she's gone now and I don't want anyone to speak of her again. She can live with the bastard and I hope she is happy." But his tone told us he didn't wish that at all, and we were shocked. We'd never before heard him curse. How could he write Fern off so easily?

"Get me some coffee, Millie. Let's get the inn going. I hope you realize this means more work for us all." And that was the end of talking about Fern. We collected ourselves and went about our day, serving the guests in the dining room and eating our own breakfasts.

Chapter 24

Father went out that morning and came back with news from the sheriff.

"Nothing. They found nothing. Foster was not on the train or any of the coaches. He's disappeared." He went upstairs to find Mother and tell her.

Johnny came by in the afternoon when he knew I might have time for tea. Felicity joined us. She was as always her sweet and gracious self and if she was feeling jealousy she betrayed no hint of it. Johnny had only a short time before he had to get back to the factory.

As he got up to leave he bent and whispered in my ear, "Is there no way we can have a visit without Felicity?" I smiled up at him and rose to push him out the door.

"Don't worry, Johnny," was all I said as I waved him down the steps to the sidewalk, but I didn't know how to fulfill his request even if I wanted to.

I had a premonition that the difficulties befalling our family were not over. When Fairy came into our room one evening before we had retired I knew something was awry. She looked worried.

"I've missed my monthly." She looked from me to Felicity, who was at the small table near the window. Felicity abruptly dropped her sewing into her lap, and I, who had been folding linens and piling them neatly into the clothes basket, fell onto the bed and nearly knocked over the basket.

We both stared and stared at her, the implication bringing on waves of concern. What of our parents who had just lost two children? Would this shock be too much for them to bear?

Felicity pointed to the chair opposite her. "Sit down, Fairy." Fairy sat, looking close to tears.

"I couldn't tell Freda or Mother. I don't know what to do."

Felicity, calmer than I would have expected, asked, "Are you sure? How long has it been?"

Fairy nodded. "It's been a couple of weeks." She looked down at her hands folded in her lap.

Felicity was becoming, like her mother, the woman of steel resolve. "What do you want to do?"

"I don't know what to do."

"Well, you know you could be pregnant. If you are do you want to keep the baby?"

Fairy looked frightened and desperate. I'm sure she never imagined that her shenanigans would bring her to this situation.

"You're too young to get married. Did you think about any of this while you were fooling around with that boy?"

Finally Fairy broke down and started to cry. "Please help me, Felicity. Can you help me?"

"I'll try." Felicity left the room with a few words addressed to Fairy. "Stay here. I'll be back in a couple minutes."

Fairy sat there, shoulders stooped, head down, not the silly arrogant child who was usually so brash. I went to her and patted her shoulder. "It will be all right. We will stand by you."

"Well, at least you don't have this problem." Her tone was slightly catty. I was surprised.

"What do you mean?"

"You know. You hardly ever get to spend time with Johnny." I was relieved to think that was what she meant.

"Yes, I am too busy. What is the boy's name?" At that she looked at me with even more concern.

"I'm not sure."

"You mean you don't know his name?" Which was worse, not knowing his name or having more than one lover? I was beginning to think that with so much of the focus on Freda too little attention had been paid to Fairy.

Fairy looked down and mumbled, "I'm not sure which one."

At this Felicity came into the room with a pot of tea and some biscuits.

"I think it best we try to help you out of this by getting rid of it. Do you agree?" I was surprised at Felicity's matter-of-fact tone.

Fairy nodded.

"Here. Drink this" She handed Fairy a cup of tea. "Then sit here and finish up the whole pot, okay?"

Fairy nodded and choked on the first big sip. She sputtered and coughed but dutifully finished the cup and then followed up with a sweet biscuit.

Felicity gave more instructions, "You will be sick later. Very sick. Tell Mother that you need to sleep in the storeroom and that way you can easily get to the privy. Use the privy and not your chamber pot. This will be easier on Millie and you might fill the chamber pot. Mother, I'm sure, will be sympathetic and get you pillows and quilts to make you comfortable. Do you understand?" Felicity waited for Fairy to nod. Fairy continued to down her tea, which must have been bitter, but she finished it along with the biscuits. Starting to look green, she got up, hugged Felicity and me, and went downstairs.

Felicity looked at me.

"I'll tell you all about it later." And we both dressed for bed, where I drew close to her warm back, grateful as Fairy said that I wouldn't have to worry about "that problem."

Chapter 25

The tea seemed to do its work. We were told the next morning that Fairy had been up all night sick and Mother stayed with her in the parlor, holding her head and applying warm damp cloths in between Fairy's trips to the privy.

Finally Fairy, having emptied everything from her digestive system, went up to her room. Since she was thirsty I was instructed to bring her tea and water, and soda crackers which Mother hoped she would be able to keep down. Both Felicity and I brought her these and some Coca-Cola too. She had moved out of her room with Freda and into Fern's old room. She looked pitiful, pale and for a teenager almost haggard. We brought warm sudsy water and cloths so she could wash up and we encouraged her to do so after she had had something to drink.

She told us in almost a whisper that nothing had happened yet and asked Felicity if it should have happened by now. Felicity told her she wasn't sure but thought it probably should have, and Fairy groaned mournfully.

We sat with her while she drank the Coca-Cola, which she said seemed to help her feel better. Then she got to her feet but was very unsteady and sat down again. Felicity wiped her sweaty face with the warm water and told her to rest while we both went back down to do the morning chores.

Mother visited her occasionally during the day and later when we had a moment Felicity and I did, yet there was no sign that the brew had worked. Although Fairy was looking better she was also becoming more distressed. Felicity tried to calm her.

That evening our supper was subdued. Fairy came down but ate very little, only playing with the small amount on her plate, but she did drink a little chicken broth we made just for her.

Our evening chores were harder. Felicity, who didn't ordinarily help, was just getting accustomed to the pattern and rhythm of work that Fern and I had developed. Mother helped and we all listened to Father as he read us the paper. There was another article about the gold rush that Father read to himself but I saw the headline when I glanced over his shoulder. Father told us the problem with the Pennsylvania Railroad had gotten more serious and now people were nervous about their money and starting to take it out of the banks and put it into gold. He was smug about having already done this himself.

Several days later when Father returned from the post office he stormed into the kitchen and bellowed for Mother, who rushed down the stairs almost falling.

"What are you so excited about, Fitzy? Why are you shouting?" Seldom did Father shout so everyone was hurrying into the kitchen to find out what had agitated him so.

"It's a letter from Foster!" And we all gathered around the kitchen table to hear what he had written.

"I've already read it but I will read it again to you." Father was so excited he was shaking.

"Dear Papa,

I know you must have been very shocked and hurt when I left but I want you to know I am safe. I'm in Saskatchewan, Canada. I've joined a group of prospectors who have a wagon train and are headed to the Yukon Territory. I have grown a beard. It's not full yet, but it should help to keep me warm in the winter and from all the stories I hear I will need it. I have warm clothes and am getting enough food, so tell Mother not to worry. I am keeping a diary of the journey and so I'll be able to share my adventures with you. I have already seen more than I would like of death as some of the group suffered from dysentery and were either left behind or died on the way. Don't worry though. I am young and healthy and will make my name when I get to the Klondike and stake a claim. Post offices are spotty and I am not sure when I can get another letter off to you. Say hello to my sisters and tell my dear Mother I love her and will be home in a year or so.

Your son,
Foster"

Mother started to cry. Father handed her the letter and she held it to her breast and wept while Father petted her hair and tried to soothe her.

The rest of us found ourselves tearing up too and after a minute Felicity filled the kettle to start tea.

"What an adventure Foster is on." Felicity tried to keep a positive outlook. "He always liked adventure. Remember, Millie, when he was climbing on the penstock after Stanley and fell off, hurting himself and ripping his pants?"

Mother looked from one of us to the other.

"When did that happen? I never heard about it." She was flabbergasted, probably more from the letter than from our story. "If you'd told us about it when it happened we might have been able to kill that adventurous spirit of his."

"Now, Flo, don't blame the girls. They were just trying to protect him too. You would have done the same yourself." Mother started to cry again as Felicity poured the tea.

Three weeks later we received a package containing a photograph of Foster, rough-looking in a hooded sheepskin coat open so we could see his breeches and suspenders. A full beard hid his cheeks and chin. It was a picture of a man and all of us had to look very closely to discern the boy we once knew.

The previous letter, which Mother carried inside her blouse, she now replaced with this new one, which said very little.

"Dear Mom and Dad,

We were getting closer to Klondike but winter has closed the pass and we are probably going to have to spend a couple of months here before we can get through. I am doing fine. If you want you can write to me here in Dawson City, Yukon, Canada. I am fine but anxious to get started again.

Hello to the girls again.

Your loving son,
Foster"

The picture was framed and put on the mantle in the parlor, and every night before she went to bed Mother would kiss it.

Chapter 26

The end came in January.

Fairy, realizing the pregnancy had not been terminated and she was starting to show, decided she had to tell our parents.

Mother took the news more easily than we would have thought. So much had been taken from her that this was not as severe a blow as losing two children.

Father on the other hand was enraged. He ranted for the whole Saturday and then made her go to the church and talk to the pastor on Sunday after the services. Father looked for every humiliation he could find to heap upon the already suffering Fairy. He didn't speak to her at supper and if he wanted something from her he would ask someone to ask her for it. He was crueler than I'd ever imagined possible from a man who had always seemed so kind and understanding.

Freda, away at school, was unaware of much of the news at the inn. Only Mother wrote to tell her of it. I wondered how proudly now she talked to her fancy friends about her home.

Economic times had become tough. Several major railroad companies had over-expanded and went into arrears. Watching seemingly solid companies going under caused panic and a run on the banks as people tried to get their money out before the bank closed down, and banks without ready cash did close. Although the inn was getting fewer guests so my chores were easier, an air of concern hung over the place. We were instructed to cut back wherever we could.

When the mortgage came due Father was without ready cash. He went to his stash of gold hidden in their bedroom under a floorboard.

We heard him yell for Mother, who went upstairs to see what the fuss was about. It was quiet for a long while.

Mother came down and went to the taproom. She went back upstairs with a bottle of brandy, picking up a glass on the way.

Fairy and I were in the kitchen preparing supper. Felicity had gone to the store. When she got back we all quietly went about our tasks, straining our ears to catch any sound.

When supper was almost ready we heard Mother and Father descending the stairs. Mother's eyes were red and her face sallow. They looked old. It was the first time I realized how old they were and that we were all getting older. The table had been set and they sat down in their regular places. We brought the food and once we were all seated Father spoke.

"We have made a sad discovery. As you all know these are hard economic times and I have carefully saved and stored our funds. Much of those savings I put into gold and hid away in our room." He gazed at Mother and reached to put his hand over hers.

"Since business at the inn is feeling the downturn I had planned to pay our mortgage with some of that gold. But that will not be possible." He paused again and Mother put her napkin to her eyes.

"When I went to get the gold I found most of it missing and a note from Foster saying he would return all of it and more when he struck gold in Klondike." Father looked down at his plate.

"So, my dears, we are ruined." He paused and heaved a great sigh. "We may have a month or two but the bank will foreclose and we will lose our business and our home." He looked around the table at each of us, even Fairy.

We were stunned. What would we do? Our home, the place where we were born and lived all of our lives, would be gone. We exchanged glances. Felicity grabbed my hand under the tablecloth and squeezed it tightly.

We ate without appetite, taking listless little bites, our minds elsewhere.

Father did not stay to read the paper that evening as we cleaned up and readied for the next day.

Anyone who came to the inn was turned away. I told the ever-patient Johnny that I wouldn't be able to visit for a while but I would send a note when things changed. He did something very odd that kept me thinking for days. He handed me two bullets, cartridges like the ones he made at the factory. He said that was how I would remember him and how he would know whether or not I had been true. I was confused by this as I had never seen another boy. But he just closed my fingers around the bullets and told me he'd be waiting for my note. It was an odd gesture, intended, I thought, to be romantic.

Father went to the bank and explained but the response was as he expected. Too many people had been defaulting and he could not be given special treatment.

We started having light breakfasts, moderate dinners and no suppers, only tea with crackers and cheese and perhaps a pie.

By the end of the week Father had made a plan. "We are going to sell the inn as is, with all the furnishings. Find a special piece of furniture you want to bring with you and pack away your personal items so we can show the place. I am leaving the box factory and we are moving to Springfield where Mother's mother still has her large house and we will move in with her." All of us looked at each other, surprised and relieved to know we would not be out on the street. But leaving a place where we had spent our whole lives would be hard.

The next day Felicity lost her mind.

It was summer again and Felicity followed me into the root cellar. With her small frame she pressed me up against the blocks of ice. "Remember when I kissed you at the picnic?" She spoke softly. "I had so wanted to be close to you and didn't know how." She paused, holding my chin so I would have to look at her she stroked my hair with her other hand. She kissed me lightly on the lips. "Now, I can't imagine losing you. I don't know what I would do." She backed away, letting me stand straight, and swept the sawdust off the back of my skirt. I picked up the lantern.

My response was probably not enough to satisfy her, "Don't worry. We're together. I will always be yours."

At supper that evening Felicity began very quietly explaining that when we got to Grandmother's she and I would still want to share a room. Mother said it wouldn't be necessary as Grandmother had lots of room for us, and wouldn't it be a treat for each of us to have our own room? Felicity insisted she could not be apart from me. Mother, Father, Fairy–all of them studied her, then me, then her again. I was shocked that Felicity was adamant about this, shocked and frightened. Felicity took my hand and said simply, "I love her and I will not be parted from her." The roof collapsed upon me, or at least that was how it felt.

Father stood up, grabbed her hand and pulled her forcefully up the stairs and locked her into our room.

When he returned he told me to sleep in the room Freda had been in. Nothing more was said as we went about our chores. Father told Fairy to see if Felicity needed anything and to get my clothes from our room.

When I went to Freda's old room, my clothes were piled on the bed, not a problem since I had so few. I could hear Felicity pacing. She knocked several times on the wall, but I was too afraid to respond. I was a coward. I could hear her talking and weeping, and talking again, and always pacing, pacing.

I was nineteen and for the first time alone in a bedroom. I cried myself to sleep.

Chapter 27

We were surprised that the bank brought potential buyers around before we were moved out.

A family called the Blacks came to look around the property. I was of course in the kitchen and could hear Mr. Black complain about nearly everything. The outside needed painting, a big job. A new roof was needed. The barn was not in good shape and might have to be torn down. A window was missing a pane. Some of the shutters were nailed shut. The plumbing was not up to date and the hand pump in the kitchen was old-fashioned, as were the gas lights since a few of the newer establishments had gone to electricity. And no telephone? How ever did we survive as an inn without a telephone? On and on went his complaints about every aspect of the old place.

All those shortcomings had gone unnoticed by us and our guests. I never thought we needed a telephone or electricity. Why, when we had all we could want for?

After several days the man from the bank paid a visit and he and Father went into the parlor to talk. They emerged about an hour later, shaking hands and saying their goodbyes.

Felicity was not coming to meals; they were brought to her. How she was managing I could not know because Mother and Fairy were the only ones allowed to take anything to her. I was too afraid and ashamed to try to talk to her, even to whisper through her door. She'd stopped tapping the wall, and was no longer pacing. I wished Fern was still with us. She would have helped, checking up and filling me in, and relaying messages.

At supper that evening Father announced that the inn was being sold to Mr. Black, who would keep running the business as an inn and boarding house.

"And Millie, you are to stay on here to work for the Blacks."

The ceiling fell again.

I sat there, stunned. My family was leaving me. I was no more than a domestic, someone to be hired and fired. I was not part of a kind and loving family.

Fairy couldn't look at me. Neither could Mother, who uncharacteristically sat slouched with her head bowed while little tears dropped into her soup. Father looked at me with a firm determination to remain immovable. He explained that it was for the best, since if he wanted to he could have us both put into an asylum. He considered it a kindness to offer me the choice of staying on with a new family in my old home and working for them or else going into an asylum. There were no other choices for me.

Felicity would go to Springfield with them or she could go into an asylum. That was her choice. Having Felicity in Springfield was to me as though she were in Africa. I couldn't get to Springfield. I would never see her again.

I got up, put my napkin down and went to my new barren room. Barren of any of my personal items, barren of any of my memories or past. Barren of Felicity.

I did not go down to help with anything. Fairy brought me coffee, eggs and toast in the morning, soup and bread at supper and tea in the evening. I had none of it. I didn't know how they were faring or who was cooking and cleaning. I drank water. I peed into the nasty chamber pot until it was almost full. I didn't know what they took or what they left. I could hear furniture scraping and scuffling about, but I just stayed in bed with my face to the wall. I had never felt so sad in my life. How could they do this to me? I had spent my whole life serving them and gotten nothing for it. That was it. I was their servant, just a convenient, cheap housemaid. I felt sorry for myself and cried and cried. When I was dried out I drank water and then some cold tea.

After three days the scuffling stopped. A note was shoved under my door, and it went quiet. Mother had written,

"Millie,
We have left for Springfield. The Blacks should arrive in a day or two. You will always be my dear daughter. Please write when you get a chance.
Love, Mother"

I went to the window to see a coach pulling away towards Depot Road.

I ran downstairs.

It looked empty. Utensils and pots were still there but anything that made it our home– pictures, calendars, little personal items–was gone.

I felt empty, as though I had gone through a serious illness. I was weak and empty. I walked through the inn, into all the rooms. All looked the same. Beds were stripped, linens folded in the closets, no personal touches remaining. I went into Mother and Father's room. Empty.

The photograph of Foster that sat on the mantle in the parlor was gone, of course.

I went into Felicity's room, my old room. Empty. The bed was stripped, but still I could smell her on the pillow. I reached under the mattress hoping to find something, but there was only mattress.

I went outside and into the root cellar. Before my lit match sputtered out I finally saw something in the sawdust and struck another match. There on the floor was an envelope.

"Dearest Millie,

My love, I am sorry our lives have been turned upside down. I am especially sorry for you, who have worked so hard for us. I never imagined our lives would end up like this. In reality I don't know how I expected them to turn out. But I am determined to come back for you.

With all my love,
Felicity"

Felicity. I kissed the letter. I cried, I pressed it to my breast and then tucked it there. Felicity loves me. She will be back. It was all I had to hold onto.

Diana K. Perkins

Part 2

Diana K. Perkins

Chapter 28

In her kindness Mother had left a gallon of milk and some cheese in the root cellar, and in the pantry a loaf of bread and some tea, sugar and flour. The chickens were still my source of eggs. I would take care of myself and live like a queen for a time and not have to cook and clean for anyone but myself. It was an oddly freeing feeling.

The Blacks arrived the next day.

Sitting quietly having my breakfast the next morning, I heard a clamor in the side yard where the coaches drove in. I went to the door and two boys ran towards it, pushed it open and ran in past me.

"Ebenezer, Ezekiel, slow down!" a woman's voice shouted. The children tore through the rooms screaming to each other.

I walked out to see a wagon piled with furniture and trunks and children.

"Hello. My name is Millie and I'm going to help you here at the inn." I didn't know what else to say. I was afraid. With so much upheaval in my life I didn't want to lose the only thing I had left, my home.

No one paid any attention to me. They were all searching through the piles of belongings on the wagon, gathering bundles, climbing up and handing things to those who had climbed down. I stepped up to the wagon and put my hands up to help. No one handed me anything so I started to untie a trunk.

"Don't touch that!" a stern disembodied woman's voice yelled at me.

"Let me help you." Finally I could see her peering over a table that had been tied down but was listing precariously.

"Here, take this." And she leaned forward with a box, passing it down to me. I carried it in.

Part of the huge pile was inside now. I decided to go to the store to get some basic groceries to feed this family, who would surely be hungry after all this moving. I walked briskly down the street and picked up cheese, a ham and more milk.

When I got home I started boiling potatoes I had found tucked in a corner of the root cellar. I planned to make a casserole as a side to the sliced ham.

The woman came into the kitchen and flopped down at the table.

"Whew! What a day. I'm tuckered." She relaxed and took a few minutes to look around. She was tall and thin with black hair pulled back severely and fashioned into a bun at the nape of her neck. A few stray strands hung like greasy strings from her temples.

"My name is Ethel, Ethel Black. Erastus, my husband, is still at the wagon unpacking. You're that Millie girl, right?" I nodded.

"So you're making supper?" I nodded again.

"Where did you get it? How are you paying for it?"

"I got it at Wellwood's, the general store. It's close by, just down the street. I put it on the inn's tab."

"You shouldn't be doing that without our permission. We have to approve everything. We need to be careful with our funds. You understand, don't you?" I nodded again.

"Sorry, I just thought you'd be hungry and…"

"I know you thought you were doing right," she interrupted me, "but you must talk to us before spending or putting anything on the inn's tab."

"Okay. I won't do it again."

The wagon was somewhat unpacked now and packages and trunks and furniture were being moved around, some left in the kitchen, some in the parlor, others distributed to their bedrooms. The family assembled in the kitchen.

A large potato casserole and sliced ham were waiting on the stove and I had set the table for supper.

Everyone sat down and introductions were made. Ethel and Erastus Black were the proud parents of two girls and three boys.

The eldest girl was Eunice and I was getting the impression her disposition was similar to Freda's though she was closer to my age. She was pretty but had a noticeable hard side. Slightly taller than me, not as thin as the others but strong, she was not a creampuff. She leaned over to shake my hand and say she was pleased to meet me.

Edith, the second eldest child, seemed more like Fern, quieter than the others, more intense and not as outgoing. She was not too bad looking, but thinner than Eunice. She wore glasses and I found out later she was like Fern in that she also loved to read.

Two girls, but no one like Felicity to comfort me.

Three boys were next. Ezekiel and Ebenezer were twins and probably around eleven years old. Everett was the youngest and I thought maybe eight.

The whole family looked like they could use a good meal or maybe a month's worth of good meals. All of them were in need of dental care and some hygienic improvements.

I put the casserole and the ham on the table and they were passed around, everyone taking a good portion. When the casserole came around to me there was very little left.

I was ready to start eating when everyone clasped their hands, bowed their heads, and said a short prayer of thanksgiving.

I was taken aback. The Whites went to church although irregularly, and celebrated the holidays, but almost never said grace. Were we the heathens while these characters were the models of religious fervor? Another reminder that the foundation of my beliefs and comfort was shaking.

Although I was reprimanded for taking the initiative to purchase and make the supper, it was obvious to me that the meal was appreciated. There was no chatter about events of the day or about their new home. Everyone simply ate and afterward the girls picked up the plates and brought them to the sink.

Ethel and Erastus and the boys disappeared upstairs while Eunice and Edith helped with the dishes. I showed them where things were and how we pumped water into the kettle and filled the reservoir and warmed it on the stove for cleaning.

When the boys and their parents returned from upstairs they told me where everyone's rooms would be. I would be sleeping with the girls in Freda and Fairy's old room, the boys would be in Foster's room and their parents would be in Mother and Father's room. The accommodations were tight with three beds squeezed into a room for two. Ethel explained that way they would be able to rent out two extra rooms.

Ethel and Erastus sat us all down at the kitchen table, to talk about rooms and plans they said. They told us we should make the best of our rooms, small as they were. They told us how they wanted us all to work together to make the inn profitable. They said they would be taking in not just guests but also boarders and they would like to get the inn as full as possible so they could afford to pay the bills. Eunice was already complaining about how much work there would be. Edith looked at me and rolled her eyes. The twins distractedly rattled the aggies in their pockets. Everett picked his nose and his parents could not have cared less.

In front of everyone Ethel said, "Millie is part of our family now, understand?" Assents and nods all around. "I want you to consider her as your sister, and Millie, I want you to call me Mother, okay?"

What else could I say? "Yes, Mother."

"Okay, Millie, do you want to show us around the inn? Where do you keep the linens? Where is a safe place to keep valuables? Erastus, do you want to see the taproom?"

And so I initiated my new family into keeping house at the Bidwell.

Chapter 29

My first night's sleep in the new room was fitful. Too much had happened in the last few weeks and with an almost empty stomach after several days of eating little, food was on my mind. I tossed and turned. Where was Freda, whose bed Eunice found perfect? Where was Fern, whose bed Edith was enjoying? What of Fairy? I made myself comfortable in her bed. Where was my dear Felicity? Foster? My family? How had this happened to us? I had been happy, or at least I thought I was. Now I was in limbo, floating freely like a lost soul with only an inn as my anchor and all these strangers invading my life and my dreams. I finally drifted off to sleep to unfamiliar breathing and snores.

The next morning I rose at my usual early hour and went to the kitchen, where Eunice, already up, seemed to be stuffing a piece of ham into her mouth as she turned away from my view. I kept silent. What could I say?

I went about my regular morning business of boiling water, making coffee, getting the bread ready for baking and visiting the chickens. I was happy the chickens were still producing enough for this ravenous family.

I started to crack and beat up a dozen eggs as Ethel came down, pinning up stray hairs and looking for an apron. I pointed towards the pantry, where the aprons hung behind the door.

"What are you doing?" Ethel asked.

"I was going to scramble up a dozen eggs for our breakfast."

"A dozen?" Her tone was alarmed.

"Yes. There are eight of us, and we should be able to stretch a dozen to feed us all."

"What did you do with yesterday's bread?"

"I gave it to the chickens. They need to be fed."

"You could have used the bread for egg toast and saved six of the eggs." Ethel was showing me how she understood the economics of inn keeping. "Then you could let the chickens out to find their own food."

"We've lost some to foxes so we've been keeping them inside their run, but I will let them out if you desire me to." I could tell she was not one to be crossed. We also didn't like to have the chickens all over the lawn and porches. My "other Mother" preferred that the inn not look like a farm with animals ranging everywhere.

When Edith came down Ethel had her write an advertisement to draw boarders to the inn:

TO LET – A pleasant, furnished room for a gentleman in a well-established Inn on Main Street in Coventry. Within a few minutes' walk of most factories. Two delightful meals included. Professionals only. Please call at the Bidwell House.

I listened to the dictation and discussion about the advertisement and wondered what previous experience they had in keeping an inn, or a boarding house.

"Have you run a boarding house?" I couldn't keep myself from asking.

My new mother responded in a tone of impatient indignation. "Why do you ask?"

"Well, your advertisement sounds very professional." I tried to sound impressed.

"We've lived in enough boarding houses to get all the experience we need. Believe me I've been had by many a thieving boarding-house keeper and now it's my turn. Not that you need to know our business. But you're part of the family now." She looked over her shoulder and gave me a strangely disquieting smile.

Every day in every way my methods of cleaning and cooking were scrutinized and "corrected." I was expected to do more with less.

We were not to wash the sheets every week but only every two weeks. Guests who were not boarders might or might not get their sheets changed depending upon how dirty we determined them to be. We brushed the bed of any hair or dirt and tucked the sheets tight so they would look like they were just put on.

We not only washed our own linens and clothes but were now taking in washing.

Fortunately I was not handy with a needle so mending the clothes, the chore that had been Felicity's, fell to Edith. She took it on with only a little grumbling.

148

The whiskey in the taproom was thinned with water, as were the milk and the cream.

Leftovers from one meal (although it was rare to have leftovers since portions were small) were used in the next meal.

Soup was watered down so it was hardly recognizable as anything but warm water. Poor little vegetables were chopped so fine they became almost a thin mush in the soup or on the plate. Rice and flour were added to thicken the thinnest versions of sauces.

A poor chicken had the very most wrung from it. Even the feet and occasionally the head (tied in muslin) were added to a soup, to be fished out before serving, and "Don't throw away the muslin, Millie."

I could only remember fondly the ham and potato casserole I'd cooked and served their first evening at the inn. That ham swirled in my memory with potatoes in a cheese and cream sauce. Some nights it permeated my dreams so much I could almost smell it.

It was not just the cooking and the washing that were scrutinized and "corrected." All aspects of the home were being guarded with a miserly eye. We were to use less wood in the woodstove, less coal in the furnace, less soap on everything.

Ethel surprised me one day when she came home with a package wrapped in paper and tied with string. I had never seen her purchase anything. What could be the wondrous new addition to our household that she so carefully handled? She summoned everyone to the kitchen and told us as she opened this precious package that we would now be subject to increasing our profits by weighing everything. The shiny new scale gleamed on the table. She showed us how to use it, warning us to be very careful not to break it.

She produced a book in which to keep records of our resources. We would be responsible for every ounce of soap or cup of flour.

I wondered how Eunice, who was clever at stealing food, would handle the scale procedure. I hoped I wouldn't be blamed for any losses that were obviously due to Eunice, who was not as thin as the rest of us.

Chapter 30

We started to attract boarders. At first they were machinists and engineer apprentices at the mills, fellows who could afford to pay for the room and board the inn provided.

Ethel had us put the first flush of these new boarders on the third floor in the ell and require them to use the back stairs. She said this was to keep the better-paying visitors in the front section, which had a nicer view of the street and the stream beyond and was more convenient to the front entrance.

Ethel had thought out how to separate the boarder dining table from the guest dining table, and she even had us put a large screen between them. That way, she thought, if more special delicacies went to the guest table the boarders would not be envious.

Gradually a lower class of worker was allowed and these we put three and four to a room. I was grateful they were allowed the use of only the privy and not any chamber pots, and they had to use the storeroom off the back to wash up. This likely saved hours of work, but still their linens were washed and their rooms swept and dusted, only not as frequently as for the others.

I was not to be at the desk; this was Erastus's duty. But I knew that the lower the fee the higher up in the inn you would be settled. The workers were in the eves with slanting ceilings so they could stand upright only in the center of the room. The ballroom, our lovely ballroom, was eventually partitioned off and made into ten tiny rooms with a hall down the middle. The walls of these rooms were of the thinnest plaster and anyone trying to put a nail into the wall to hang his jacket would find it not holding but rather tearing the wall apart, for which they would be fined.

Ethel and Erastus made the most of their investment, and with the tightest of reins on the purse they must have been able to save a tidy sum. But they complained all the while about the cost of food and wood and coal and were miserly about every expense. We received no pay for our work since, as Ethel pointed out, we were given a roof over our heads and food and warmth and so we should be paying them. But she said that only when Eunice or Edith complained. It was mentioned that since I was part of the family I certainly wouldn't be getting any more share in the profit than any of the others.

Ezekiel and Ebenezer found work at one of the factories sweeping and doing odd jobs. They were allowed to keep a small percentage of their salaries, with the rest disappearing into the deep pockets of Ethel and Erastus.

Everett ran wild and was barely to be seen except at breakfast and supper. I think he spent most of his time at the lake because I sometimes found fish-hooks and string in his pockets when I was washing his clothes.

Of all the family I liked Everett the best. He seemed the one least affected by the rest of the family's stingy mindset. Lighthearted and laughing, he ignored most of the rules the elder Blacks imposed upon us. He smiled at me and made jokes. The miserly ways that seemed to extend even to happiness, which was usually in short supply, did not settle into Everett.

Every Sunday the whole family put on their nicest clothes, which were not what most people would consider nice but were the best they had, and trooped off to the Methodist church. I, as a Congregationalist, was not to go with them but was expected to stay home and have Sunday dinner ready when they returned, famished and irritable.

Erastus had bought us some turkeys and one of these would be slaughtered every weekend for the Sunday dinner. This was a great treat for all of us since it was the largest meal we would enjoy all week.

With Edith's help I had started a garden in the side yard that added a little more sustenance to our meager meals, but still most went to the guests and boarders.

Thankfully Eunice did some of the kitchen work, so she could pinch food I'm sure, but I was grateful for the help nonetheless.

And Edith helped with laundry and room chores, but with more guests than the Whites had ever had I was still overburdened with work. Sometimes Edith would disappear and I'd find her curled up in a corner reading a book. She would apologize but say she needed to rest now and then. I asked her what she was reading and she said this was a new novel just out and quite frightening. *Dracula* was its title.

I realized I worked harder than anyone else and I didn't know how long I would be able to, or how long I wanted to. My knees were a constant red scab, my hands always raw and my arms mottled from rough soap. I must have looked a mess. Loose strands of hair dangled into my face, rags of clothes hung from me and my apron drooped from my thin frame. When I glimpsed myself in one of the guest room mirrors I was shocked at how unkempt and pathetic I looked. When had this happened? Who had I become? What could I do? I had been told I needed to work for the Blacks for at least two years, as part of the agreement in the purchase of the inn. But how could they handle me like property? I had not seen the agreement, nor did I know what was legal and lawful.

In the six months since the Whites had moved I had tried to write to Felicity. I knew the Whites were in Springfield and the postmaster gave me the forwarding address. But all the letters came back to me with "Not at this address" written on them. I didn't know if the address was wrong or if Felicity was not there or if my other mother and father were sending them back. I had no idea what was going on until one day I got a letter from Fern.

Chapter 31

Fern had eloped with Harold Jenkins. They lived nearby in Mansfield where he had taken a teaching position at the school. Originally they had escaped to Vermont and married as soon as they could, afraid that if caught Fern would be forced to go back home. She said she was happy. News about the inn had gotten to her and she was shocked. She felt bad for me since she thought they had taken advantage of me. I had been ill-used and now to have to work for the Blacks seemed unfair to her. She had maintained some acquaintances in town and she said the information they gave her about the mills and the inn saddened her. She was surprised to hear that the inn had gone so much downhill in such a short time. She said our parents were keeping Fairy at home and telling everyone she had been married and her husband had abandoned her. Felicity was home too. Freda was engaged to be married to a banker from Springfield in about a year. But that was the extent of the news.

After reading her letter I looked around and realized the inn did look shabby. The paint was peeling, the grass grown high, the flowerbeds gone to weed. The only garden that looked decent was my patch of vegetables. Chickens ran everywhere and the turkey pen was barren of any blade of grass or scrap of green, and on hot muggy days it could be smelled from the lawn where we had chairs set up for guests. Erastus was doing a booming business in the saloon, which was no longer the quiet gentlemanly taproom Father ran, but instead enticed a dirty, drunken crowd prone to cursing and brawling.

If Father and Mother could see what had so quickly happened to this jewel on the main street, they would probably have cried.

I was exhausted and wondered how I could escape from the bondage that had become my life. I could run away but had nowhere to go. I could start to see Johnny, who had made it known he was carrying a torch for me. That would be the simplest escape, but what would we do? Get married? Where would we move to? He was still living at home and couldn't afford to get a place of his own. Would we have to live with his parents? What sort of an escape would that be?

The day after I received the letter from Fern I stole a few minutes to start planning my escape. In my best clothes, which no longer fit but hung from my gaunt frame, I walked briskly down to Mason's Cartridge Factory where Johnny worked. A bunch of the fellows were sitting on the steps eating lunch and I could hear them calling to Johnny in a teasing tone. He responded, peering out the door, wiping his hands on his leather apron. He came down the steps, greeting me with a smile, and turned me around to walk me back up the road, away from the group on the steps.

"I know you haven't seen me in months. I have been so busy at the inn with the Blacks running everything," I started to explain.

He shushed me as he stopped and looked at me.

"I know you've been busy. I wasn't sure if I should wait or not. I didn't know if you were interested in me or if you were just looking for company."

I took the two cartridges out of my pocket and handed them to him. "I may not have seen you but I didn't forget you." He was a nice boy, and a machinist. I probably wouldn't be able to do better. He was handsome, with curly dark hair, a nice smile and dimpled cheeks. I just needed to get away from my life at the inn and this seemed like the only way. I hoped he could see what I was offering.

"Can I come by this evening? When do you think you'll have time to visit?"

"I really don't finish up my chores until around ten. Can you come by that late? Maybe we can visit as I knead the bread for tomorrow's breakfast. If you're there at eight I may be able to have a cup of tea. Will you come?"

"Yes, I'll stop in around eight. I'm glad you remembered me. I was starting to lose hope." He gave me a light hug, trying not to get me dirty.

We both walked briskly back to our duties, I to the inn's drudgery, he to his work at the factory.

The cartridge factory was no longer owned by Mason even though everyone still called it Mason's, its original name. Then it became the Phoenix Metallic Cartridge Company, and later the American Metallic Cartridge Company. Johnny did some mechanical work there, fixing machines, but his primary job was crimping the cartridges once they had been loaded. He ran the machine that compressed the edge of the shell firmly around the ball. This was dangerous, specialized work and he was paid well for it.

The original cartridge factory was well-known for supplying a large number of cartridges to the Union Army during the Civil War. Since then demand had dropped but the forward-thinking Henry Mason realized that the push west and the needs of hunters still offered a good market for dependable standardized cartridges. Mason had about thirty hands at the factory, all employed in some form of cartridge-making. He was a good employer and turnover was rare. So for me Johnny was an easy choice. I knew he would be a good provider. But I couldn't understand why with his earnings he was still at home. Perhaps, I hoped, he was amassing hefty savings.

Chapter 32

That evening Johnny came by earlier than expected. I was surprised to see that instead of stopping in the kitchen to visit with me, and Edith, he said hello but went through to the taproom to spend time with Erastus.

I'd finished my chores, rushing more than usual, and it was getting towards ten when I went into the taproom to find him.

The room was dark, lit only by a few lights over the little bar and several candles on the tables.

I didn't see Johnny right off. I looked to Erastus behind the bar, who pointed at Johnny slumped over a table, seemingly asleep. I went over and shook his shoulder and he almost fell off the chair onto the floor, but he righted himself and looked up at me bleary-eyed, rubbing his face with his hand.

"Whoops, sorry. I must have fallen asleep waiting for you." He apologized in a thick voice and stood up, one hand steadying himself on the table. Walking slowly to the bar, he leaned across it and said softly, "Thanks for taking care of me, Erastus." He pulled several coins from his pocket and pushed them across the bar towards the man, who brushed them into his hand.

"No problem, Johnny." This was all done in a most casual manner as though it was a common interchange between them.

I followed him into the kitchen, where he stopped and leaned his back against the table, asking, "What do you

159

say? How about some tea?" He looked at me, squinting with one eye closed.

"Maybe another time or maybe I can get an afternoon off and we can go out for a picnic." I was distressed by his drunkenness and didn't want to spend time with him like this.

"Okay, okay, you come by when you can figure it out, but remember, I'm not going to wait forever." He lurched towards the door.

"Okay, Johnny, I'll come by and tell you when I can get an afternoon off." He didn't say goodbye, just stumbled down the steps to the sidewalk. I watched as he headed towards his home, thankful it wasn't far away. I was surprised by the end of the evening. I'd thought he was still interested in me but now I felt I wasn't foremost in his mind. I was discouraged but still determined.

The next day I asked Ethel if I could get some time off. I was hoping this was just a common event, Johnny in his cups.

Ethel was surprised. I'd never asked for time off. I imagined that Erastus had told her about Johnny in the taproom the previous night.

"Whatever would you need time off for?" Ethel's sideways glance told me she knew and was just going to make it hard for me.

"I only want an afternoon off. I want to go on a picnic with Johnny. I would like Sunday when he has the time off too."

"A picnic with Johnny? Johnny Knight the machinist? Really? What would he want with a scullery maid?"

"What?" I could hardly believe I was hearing her right, it was such a mean comment. "Is that what you think of me? I'm your scullery maid?"

"Don't get uppity with me, Millicent Submit. That is your middle name, right? Submit?"

"That's what I was named. Yes."

"Well, don't get so uppity with me. I have your papers and I won't release you until you've finished your indenture." Ethel's lips were thin and firmly pressed together.

"What do you mean, my indenture?"

"That was part of the deal with the Whites. Didn't you know?" Her question had a cruel twist to it.

"No, I didn't know. What do you mean?" I couldn't imagine I would be required to work against my will. "I never signed anything."

"As long as you were the Whites' ward and were not of age, they had the right to contract you to us."

"That's impossible." I couldn't imagine it.

"Not only is it possible but I have the signed contract." She paused, then continued in a reedy whining voice, "But if you have the vanity to believe that Johnny Knight, a skilled machinist, would be interested in someone of your lowly caliber, I'll let you have an afternoon to find out." She drew herself up to her full skinny height. "You see, I can be kind or I can be cruel. It all depends on you."

I didn't know how to respond. She would give me an afternoon off, but surely I deserved it. I had worked non-stop for months, eaten their miserable gruel, frozen in that room during the winter and now sweated in the summer. I was angry but I was too off-guard to figure out the best way to respond. She had me.

"Thank you." I was bested, weakened by months of near starvation. I had been hoping the afternoon with Johnny would prove so successful I could escape my sad predicament.

"But remember, you won't be getting out of this contract for another year and a half, so don't imagine that you'll marry and leave us in the lurch." She knew what I was hoping for and was quietly blocking my escape. "You're going on a picnic? Where do you think you'll get your picnic lunch? Not from our larder, I hope. We can't spare you a lunch to help you bait your hook."

Ethel. Her name so reminded me of the harsh spirits in some of Father's drinks. Harsh and bitter and coarse.

Chapter 33

I ran off when no one was around and rushed to tell Johnny we could picnic the next Sunday.

That Saturday I went to the market with some of the limited amount of money I'd saved when the Whites were paying us. I picked up a small salami, a wedge of cheese and a large rye bread, some early apples and a couple pints of beer. This was more money than I had ever spent on myself. The man at the market threw in a couple of pickles and smiled knowingly. "Picnic, eh?" I nodded. "There's a pretty spot up by the lake that's nice for that and private. Hardly anyone goes there, but it's best to cut through the cemetery. Sometimes fishermen are there but it's a fine spot." I thanked him and packed the goods into my satchel.

The next day the family went off to their regular Sunday services. Looking pious and self-righteous, Ethel turned to me as she went out the door.

"Remember, I've weighed everything…"

"Don't worry. I have my own picnic purchased already." I was tempted to stick my tongue out and say I would probably eat better that afternoon than I had in months, but I stayed silent.

"Have fun," she said sarcastically. "And don't get into any trouble." She emphasized the word 'trouble' nastily.

I just waved her goodbye.

I ran around gathering our picnic lunch, a small cutting board, a knife, a bottle opener, some napkins and a tablecloth all wrapped and tucked lovingly into my basket. Even with my mean guardian watching to oversee me, I was actually anticipating this with excitement.

I left behind a cold roast and cole salad for the family when they returned. They would be miss their customary turkey dinner yet still dine well. But you could be sure anything left over would be put towards the next meal and the next day's meals and the day after that if they could stretch it that far.

The poor fare at the inn had gradually discouraged all but the meanest workers, those who could afford to go nowhere else. Poor buggers, I thought, they were hardly better off than I.

I was prepared long before the appointed hour and wandered about the kitchen tidying up absentmindedly, trying to be patient and not get overly excited lest I be disappointed.

Finally Johnny arrived and hugged me and kissed me on the cheek. I gathered up our basket and my hat and a blanket and we headed out. Johnny carried the basket as we climbed the hill to the lake, and I told him about the spot the man at the market had suggested. He said he knew of it and we headed towards the path. After walking respectfully through the cemetery, we found steps that dropped down to a well-worn trail along the shore. It led away from the water and we had to duck under branches and around bushes. Finally we came to a wide flat opening on a secluded ledge overlooking the water.

Johnny spread out the blanket and I spread the tablecloth on it and laid out our sumptuous lunch. I felt like

I was in a dream: a beautiful spot, no work to do, an abundance of good food and a nice man to share it with. Of course always looming over me was the fact that this bubble would burst in a few hours when I would have to go back to the inn and work twice as hard to make up for taking a few hours off.

We cut into the salami and cheese and took a few bites before we slowed down to a leisurely enjoyment of our picnic. Johnny told me stories about the fellows he worked with and some of their exploits. He said one of the boys lived on a farm up on Cooper Lane and one day when he and some of his friends were bored they ran the hay wagon down the hill. It went like lightning the boy said and they couldn't control it but fortunately the wagon and all of them came out unscathed, although frightened enough not to attempt that again. Then they had to haul it back up the hill. Johnny talked about fishing and hunting and a little about his brother and his parents, although I sensed this was not the most engaging topic for him. Generally he seemed like a happy guy as he smiled and laughed a fair amount and drank his beer quickly and then asked if I wanted the other. When I told him I wanted only the few sips I'd already had he polished off the remainder.

We were sated and warm in the sun. He lay on his back and motioned for me to lie next to him. So I did and lay on my back with my head in the crook of his arm. I felt very comfortable and could have fallen asleep were it not for the tension between us, the tension of the anticipation of something about to happen. I expected him to kiss me. I think I wanted him to, but I was also afraid of it, afraid of what else might happen. I lay very still, waiting, unable to relax. Finally he spoke.

"What do you want, Millie?" A simple question.

"I don't know, Johnny."

"Do you want me to kiss you?" It seemed strange. I remembered Foster. He hadn't hesitated. He'd declared his love, tried to kiss me whether I wanted him to or not.

I wasn't sure what my response should be. "Do you want to kiss me, Johnny?"

"You're a tease, Miss Millie." He pulled me onto him and started to tickle me. I giggled and squirmed.

"I think you do want me to kiss you." He rolled on top of me and kissed me. Not the gentle sensuous kiss I would have imagined but a hard, messy kiss, trying to push his tongue into my mouth. This was what I had expected but I didn't exactly like it. I tried to wriggle out from under him. But he held me fast and continued to kiss my lips, then my cheek and my ear and my neck. I started to fight him.

"Enough. That's enough," I said with a note of fear and urgency. He was gentleman enough to stop, and rolled off me.

"Sorry. I thought you wanted me to..." He sounded a little insulted, a little misunderstood.

"I do, but not like that." I didn't know how else to explain it.

"How then? Don't you like my kisses? You haven't been out with another boy, have you?"

"Of course not. When would I ever have the chance to go out with anyone else? Why would I want to see anyone else, Johnny?" This seemed to satisfy him. "Maybe we should just wait a little longer before we go any further."

"Wait? Until when? When will you get another day off? I hardly see you now, and it's not because I don't want to, it's because you're too busy."

"I know, I know. Maybe we can meet after I finish my chores like we did last week."

"I can't wait that late every night. I have to go to work." He sounded exasperated.

"I'm sorry. I don't know what else to do. I can't leave. I still owe the Blacks some time. They have me under contract for another eighteen months."

"Really? Eighteen months? How did they manage that?" Johnny was surprised.

"It's something the Whites worked out with them before they left."

"What if we got married?" It was probably out of his mouth before he even realized what he'd said.

"What?" Although it had been playing through my mind, I wasn't expecting him to offer it so casually.

He realized he'd moved ahead more quickly than either of us was prepared for. "Well, I was just thinking it might help to get you out of your contract. I mean, would you like to marry me?"

"Are you proposing, Johnny Knight?"

"Well, yes, I'm proposing to you, Miss Millicent Submit White." He sat up and pulled me to my knees. He knelt before me on one knee and took my hand. "Will you marry me?"

I stared at him, dumbfounded.

"I have no ring to offer you, but I do have the two cartridges. Will you take one as my promise to marry you?"

My mind was whirling. Things were all happening so fast. I did want to escape from the inn. I did want to marry him. What choice did I have? He was a good man with a good job, and I would be lucky to get him. He waited, holding my hand.

"Yes, Johnny Knight, I would be happy to be your wife." And he pulled me close and kissed me again.

Chapter 34

When we returned to the inn the Black family was of course already home and had had themselves a nice meal. The girls had piled the dishes in the sink.

Everett came running into the kitchen singing "Johnny and Millie, sitting in a tree, k-i-s-s-i-n-g." Ethel told him to be quiet and go outside and get the eggs from the chickens. He stopped singing, took the egg basket and walked solemnly out the door.

Johnny and I had practiced what we would do. Johnny was going to find Erastus and ask him for my hand. So he asked Ethel where Erastus was and Ethel told him in the taproom. Johnny disappeared down the hall towards it.

I busied myself helping with the dishes, not saying a word to anyone. I thought I could feel them burning with questions. Finally when Ethel went into the pantry Edith whispered, "Well, what happened? Did you have a good time?" Edith was a little younger than me and probably feeling as constrained by this family as the rest of us. What fun did she have? Only snatching a few minutes here or there to read her book. She wasn't a bad sort. I was sure the Blacks were keeping their eyes peeled for appropriate suitors for their daughters. Edith was average-looking but thin and wore glasses. Still, she might be able to attract a nice boy if she were ever allowed to get out.

"He asked me to marry him." I was so self-satisfied and I wanted her to know there was an escape from this bondage. She almost dropped the plate she was drying and caught it just in time.

"Really?" She actually sounded pleased.

"Yes, really. And I said yes."

"Do you really like him? Do you love him?" Such simple questions, for which I had no ready answer.

"Well, we've been seeing each other on and off for over a year. He really is very nice, and he has a good job." I was avoiding the question and Edith knew it.

"Yes, but do you love him?"

"I'm not sure. I'm not sure if I know what love is." Was I lying to myself? Did I know what love was?

"Well," she said, satisfied, "I don't think we always know what it is. And I don't know if people who marry are always in love. Maybe it's something you grow into." Though younger she had wise insight. I nodded. She asked me for details. What did we have to eat? Where did we go? Did he kiss me? Did he get down on one knee? She was living vicariously through me and I was fine with that. After that evening Edith and I grew closer and she often made the time to do chores with me. She'd talk about what books she was reading and which boys were looking at her in church.

I was growing concerned because Johnny hadn't come right back from the taproom. Either Erastus needed some convincing or Johnny had lost his nerve, or maybe he'd had another evening of too much beer. Soon they both appeared. Erastus clapped Johnny loudly on the back. "Well, my boy, we'll be welcoming you into our happy home. Remember, you can call *me* Dad too." I was grateful no one else was in the kitchen to watch Erastus come over and give me a big hug. I could see Johnny behind him. He shrugged at me.

"Congratulations, Millie. You've got yourself a winner here." And he clapped Johnny on the back again. Johnny smiled at him and shook his hand and kissed me on the cheek.

"I'm the lucky one," Johnny said as he headed towards the door. I could smell the alcohol on him and thought he might have been celebrating, but not too much. He waved at me and went out the door and down the sidewalk, whistling

"We'll talk about all this in the morning, all right, Millie?" Erastus had been celebrating too. He headed upstairs and I was left in the kitchen to knead the bread and think about this very full day.

Was this a mistake? Was I rushing into this because I was so tired of the drudgery at the inn? Were there other ways for me to escape? Could I get a job at one of the factories? Lots of women worked there. Could I have survived another eighteen months under the vigilant gaze and tight purse of the Blacks?

Through the months since the Whites left I'd been writing Felicity, and Fern. All of Felicity's letters were returned unopened but Fern would occasionally send news of the family who had left me behind. Fairy had been writing to Fern and kept her informed about the events at home. Fern wrote that Fairy had a baby boy and our parents let her keep him because when they had threatened to take him away Fairy became severely despondent and stopped eating. Fern said our parents were adjusting and actually enjoying having a grandson. Fern was pregnant also and both she and her new husband were looking forward to starting a family. There was little about Felicity except she was home and more withdrawn. Father was bringing boys home from the factory in Springfield where he had gotten a new position, but Felicity so far showed no interest. No word of Foster.

I wrote to Fern that I had a beau who had proposed to me and I had accepted. I told her a little about Johnny. I wrote about the Blacks and how different it was from when our parents ran the place. And I told her how much I thought the inn had gone downhill in such a short time. I asked her to send my love to everyone and to tell Felicity I thought of her daily.

Ethel and Erastus came down to the kitchen together. The bread had wafted its wonderful scent upstairs as it did every day inviting all to breakfast. The boarders had already been served their meal and their plates awaited washing. I was starting the egg toast when the senior Blacks made their entrance. They said good morning and sat down quietly, appearing unusually subdued. I was waiting for the attack, anticipating a rough time.

"Well, my lady, you were able to catch him, huh?" Ethel couldn't hold herself back.

"Now, Ethel, remember we said we would be nice."

"I am being nice," she replied in her whiny nasal voice. "She's the one who's trying to break the contract."

Erastus chimed in. "You're not planning to break the contract now, are you, Millie? I don't think she'd do that, Ethel."

"If you try to break the contract you will be indebted to us for the year and a half's wages that we will need to pay anyone we hire to replace you." Ethel was firm. "Do you understand?"

Erastus was again trying to make the best of things. "I'm sure we can work something out, Ethel. Why, maybe she could continue to work and live here with Johnny." He looked at me, nodding, then turned his gaze to Ethel. "Maybe Johnny could even help around here for his room and board." He nodded again, looking from Ethel to me and back again. I was getting the sense that they had this little vignette all planned before they came down. Two servants. That would work out just fine for them.

"I don't know if we could do that." Ethel was playing her part. "Nothing like that is in the contract. We would probably have to rewrite it and extend it for another year."

I couldn't let this go any further.

"Let me talk to Johnny and see if he would agree. If he doesn't we may have to wait until my contract is up." There. If I let them know I could wait, I might have more to barter with.

"I hinted to Johnny about it last night," Erastus chimed in. "I think he might be willing."

I thought they were trying to nail me down, trying to get me to commit to something before talking to Johnny, but I wasn't going to be persuaded.

"I'll talk to him about it."

Surprisingly Ethel was much nicer for the rest of the day. I would have to catch Johnny before he got to the taproom tonight. Who knew how easily swayed he was once he had a few drinks?

The Blacks. I thought it a bitter irony that my first family was kind and honest and as generous as they could be and they were named White, while this Black family was mean and miserly. How fitting the names were, how strange. I felt I was becoming cheap like them, counting up their small cruelties, watching how much each ate, how much they spent. I was becoming something I never would have expected, sly and cautious and sneaky. I didn't like these changes in myself, but I felt it was the only way I could survive in this new environment. Be wary, Millie, I told myself. Be cautious. They may say I am one of the family, but that has been said before by a better family than this.

Chapter 35

I was grateful that Johnny arrived while I was still doing chores, giving me the chance to talk to him before the Blacks could. Edith kindly told me she would finish up the dishes so I could go out back with him. I lit a lantern and took him by the hand to the root cellar, where I believed no one would see us while we conversed privately for a few minutes.

I barely greeted him with a quick hug and kiss before I blurted out, "Johnny, I only have a couple of minutes before I must get back, but I need to know what Erastus talked to you about last night." I was almost breathless, rushing to get to the point. He understood, nodding.

"Well, I told him I had asked you to marry me. He didn't seem too surprised and he immediately offered me a little shot of brandy to 'celebrate' he said. Then, as he has been doing, he continued my tab and poured me a beer. He told me you were a catch and I would be lucky to get such a hard-working gal, but then he went right into how perhaps I might do better with the daughter of the innkeeper... and he gave me a sly smile and a wink. I was, obviously, surprised. He quickly gauged my response and said he understood that you were obviously the one for me."

Johnny saw that I was as surprised as he, and he went on. "Can you believe his gall? So he started down another tack, saying they couldn't let you out of their contract, which he thought might go on for another sixteen or eighteen months, so we might need to wait that long before we could wed. Erastus paused there, again checking my response. I didn't want him to think it bothered me one way or the other. I was waiting for his next proposal since it seemed he was about to offer up something else."

I was surprised and well-pleased by Johnny's shrewdness, and also bristling at the duplicity of these professed second parents of mine. I was so excitedly anticipating the rest of his story that I grabbed his hands. "Then what? What did he say next?"

"Well, I had finished off that beer and he quickly poured me another, smiling broadly. 'What do you think about wedding Millie and living here with her for a while, until of course her contract is up?' I took it all in and he quickly rejoined, 'You could help us too. We could give you a small stipend, but because you'd be getting room and board for free, we couldn't give you much.' That was his offer to me, to us. I was careful not to have too many beers and agree to something that might not be in our best interest." Johnny seemed proud that he'd remembered the whole interchange and all of its nuances and had been careful enough not to commit to anything.

"I knew it!" I exclaimed. "They both approached me this morning saying as much. They are so sly." I hugged him again and kissed him on the cheek. "You were perfect. What do you think we should do?" He looked pleased.

"I'm not sure. I'm not sure I want to get wrapped into this contract or commitment that you've found yourself in." Johnny was wisely cautious.

"I don't blame you. If I knew how I could get myself out before the appointed time I would leave today."

"But then again, I'm not sure I want to wait a year and a half to marry you." He had taken my hand and he was smiling. "Maybe I can get an attorney to draft up an agreement that they won't be able to twist into something more."

I shrugged. "You think you can move in and live here with me and do some work for them and when my contract is up we can both leave? You'd want to do that?"

"Well, I don't really want to do that, but if it means we can wed sooner, I'd be willing."

"Really? Do you know an attorney?"

"There is one who represents the cartridge factory. I see him come in now and again. I could talk to him."

"Okay, if that's what you think. I've got to get back in before someone discovers I'm gone. Edith was covering for me. I'm grateful to her." I picked up the lantern, which was throwing strange shadows on the walls and the boxes of stores.

We kissed again and he followed me into the inn and sat at the kitchen table drinking tea while I started the bread for the next day.

I was excited to think I might be getting some relief from the work here. At least I'd have a companion to share the burden of my bondage, someone to commiserate with over the harsh demands of my master and mistress.

While I was kneading the dough Ethel came down. Upon seeing Johnny she spoke in her usual cutting nasal voice but tried to give a pleasant lilt to it. "Well, did you decide what you were going to do?" Johnny and I exchanged glances. Johnny replied.

"No, we haven't decided yet. Can we tell you next week?"

Ethel seemed a little surprised. "You haven't decided yet? Well, when do you think you will? We've been thinking of taking on a man. You'd better decide soon."

I thought she was lying. I'd never heard them talk of taking on another person. I imagined this was just a way to pressure Johnny into agreeing sooner before he changed his mind altogether.

"Why don't you go visit Erastus? He's in the taproom and I'm sure he'd like to see you." The invitation was as sweet as she could make it in her edgy voice. I imagined they could charge him for the beer but not for the tea, and that tight purse was what ran this even tighter innkeeper. Even her mouth was drawn in like the tightly clamped purse. I'd never noticed how much she looked like a sly fox, eyes shifting between Johnny and me, mouth working, body alert, thin lips barely stretched over poorly kept teeth. I got a sudden chill and the hair on my neck stood on end. This woman, I thought, is cunning and evil. Johnny must have read my mind because he backed away from her.

"Yes, I think I'll go visit him." He left and she turned to me.

"Whatever it is you two are cooking up, just forget it. We have your contract and we're keeping you to it. Do you understand?" She was firm and the gentler tone she'd used with Johnny was gone.

She stood there waiting.

"Do you understand?" She was determined to get an answer from me.

"Oh, yes, Mother, I understand," I said very sweetly. She snapped back as though I'd struck her.

"Good." Her reply wasn't as firm as she likely wanted it to be. I think it was dawning on her that I might be more formidable than she'd imagined. She left the room.

Chapter 36

When Johnny came back out through the kitchen and gave me a kiss on the cheek as he went out the door, Erastus followed him and waved goodbye.

"I hope you two aren't plotting anything." His tone was slightly threatening. "Ethel is not one to go up against."

"Why would we do that, dear Father?" My voice so sweet it must have been obvious I was not sincere. He didn't even say goodnight as he went up the stairs to join his wife.

I poured myself tea and sat alone in the quiet kitchen, thinking about the evening and wondering what we would do and how we could make it through this without becoming more deeply entangled with this family.

I decided that tomorrow when I had a free moment like this I would write Fern and tell her about the mess here. Perhaps she would have some ideas about how to break the contract.

I stayed up late the next night writing page after page to Fern. Johnny had come by to say he was seeing the attorney the next week and he didn't want to face Erastus or Ethel again until after he knew more. He thought it too unpleasant. I understood and agreed. I was beginning to think that conflict was what fed these people and without it they seemed somewhat starved for energy. When I agreed with them and didn't offer any resistance they didn't know what to do. So I went along, or seemed to, with everything.

Even if I didn't agree I pretended to. If at some point in the future I was going to rebel this would give me the reserve, the saved-up vigor, to employ in our psychic battle. Our opponents seemed to believe we had surrendered, or at least they didn't understand we were regrouping, and the inn was quiet for a week.

During the hiatus the twins Ezekiel and Ebenezer provided the biggest excitement. They had been working at the Woods Mill, which made cotton and fine wool doeskin, for almost all the nine months since they'd moved here. They had started out sweeping up the fine dust motes that collected daily under the machines. They were smart and watched the people work and were soon helping to dress the looms, weaving the fine warp threads through the metal heddles. The job was tedious, and the weavers found it a great help to have the pair's small fingers and good eyesight that enabled them to get inside the loom and pull the warp threads through. The boys became very proficient at it, and although they were not allowed to run the power looms the weavers fought over access to their services.

This was all very good for the twins, who were getting regular work and also several raises. They would likely have landed permanent jobs there once they finished school if they hadn't caused trouble.

One of the weavers was having difficulty. This particular weaver was not the fastest on the floor, but she was fastidious and a favorite of the boss because her work was almost always perfect, so that what she lacked in speed she made up for in quality. The fine fabric coming from her looms was given a quick check, as was all outgoing product, and hers never had to be relegated to a second-class pile that could not command the best price. For some reason the twins took a dislike to her. They picked on her, not by mis-threading the warp, which might be noticed as their work, but by putting in an occasional weak warp thread. The warp threads hold the weight of the fabric as it is woven, so a weak thread endangers the whole piece; if it breaks it is difficult to fix without a noticeable repair. A good dresser would notice a weak warp thread or one which varied in thickness, and reject it as unacceptable. Why the boys imagined they would not be blamed for sabotaging the warp of this particular weaver was beyond my comprehension.

After they ruined several of her pieces the floor manager came down to inspect the loom and talk to her. This attention caused them to back off for a while, but after a couple more weeks they again began to dress the loom with some of the discards. This time the weaver caught it. She didn't talk to the twins but went to the manager and pointed out the problem, which could only have been deliberate.

The manager summoned both boys to the office and asked them about the dressing of that loom. They said it must have been an oversight but he didn't believe them. They accused the weaver of not liking them and trying to get them fired. Finally the floor manager called in the department manager and the weaver too. The twins began to realize their actions wouldn't be seen as poor work on their part but as malicious attempts to discredit the weaver, and they had caused the loss of quality pieces and cost the company money they might be required to pay back. This was looking serious.

In the end they were fired and not only denied recommendations but also an unfavorable report would follow them to any jobs they might apply for in the future. By tomorrow the news would be all over town and no employer would hire them.

When Edith heard about it she was very curious as to why the boys would be so mean. The twins told their version of the story, that the weaver was incompetent but blamed the shoddy work on them. But information was leaking back to us through a number of other sources. Johnny was one. We decided he should talk to the weaver to learn more, approaching her carefully but not confronting her.

When he waited on the road by the Woods Mill he spotted someone he thought might be the weaver. She was tall and spare and looked so much like Ethel he thought at first it was. He immediately understood the twins' intense dislike of the woman, who was speaking to someone in the same high tinny voice Ethel had. When Johnny told us we laughed. But it wasn't really funny. Ethel had poisoned her children and was on her way to ruining their lives.

When Ethel heard the boys had been fired she lost her temper. Her thin lips worked repeatedly from a grimace to a pucker. She was trying to hold her wrath in check but we could almost see the steam puffing out of her ears. With her black stringy hair pulled back so severely, her pointed nose looked like an arrow aimed at the boys. She insulted them and came close to striking them with a hickory switch before Erastus interrupted and tried to calm her down.

It was the beginning of a wave of calamities that washed the Blacks out of the inn.

Chapter 37

After Johnny spoke to the attorney we decided to try to stay at the inn. We couldn't afford to write a special contract so we were going to agree to work at the inn for the remaining sixteen months and then figure out what to do after that. We hadn't told the Blacks yet.

When I picked up the mail at the post office I found a fat letter from Fern. I could hardly wait to open it but didn't get the chance until after supper when my chores were done and everyone had gone to bed. I was grateful tonight that Johnny hadn't come by as I spread the pages on the table and started to read. There was news of Fairy and her baby, of our parents, of Fern's husband's promotion, and of Felicity, who on hearing that I was to be wed, had a breakdown and was put into a hospital. If she improved, Fern said, she was to go to a nice school for young women in Northampton, Massachusetts.

This news pained me. My heart was heavy with the thought of hurting Felicity and of her hospital confinement. I felt powerless. What could I do to help? I had no money, I had no idea even where Springfield was, except that it was a rail stop north of us. How could I get there to see her, to tell her that I had no choice but to wed? Flashes of memories came into my mind: the time Freda caused Felicity to hurt herself with the needle, the day I gave her the thimble, sitting in the circle of light quietly having tea and reading while she sewed. The memories plunged me into such sadness that it was quite a while before I could pick up the letter again and continue reading.

Fern said she'd visited our parents. They hadn't refused to see her but rather were very kind to her, inviting her to supper and asking about her new life. She was very surprised and pleased to see them and share the latest news. The visit was so pleasant it was not until she was almost ready to leave that she remembered to tell them about my engagement and about the contract the Blacks had me under. That small bit of information caused her to miss her train because a long discussion ensued. The Whites said they had no knowledge of a contract and had never signed such a thing. They had agreed to allow me to stay and work until the Blacks felt confident could run the inn and afterward they would have to find lodging for me or take me on at a higher rate–a higher rate because they were to be paying me for the help I was providing.

Fern said she read parts of my letters to them and they were appalled at my mistreatment and how the Blacks had abused the agreement made during of the purchase of the inn.

I was flabbergasted. I poured myself more tea and reread the whole letter and then reread the part about the contract over and over. I was angry and excited. I had nothing to break, no contract, and I was in fact owed back wages!

How could this be? How could these *good* people be so bold as to swindle a young woman?

Maybe I could take my wages and travel to Springfield.

I stayed up long past midnight, excitedly reading and pacing and yearning to tell Johnny and Edith, who would probably be excited too. I rarely saw Eunice these days since we had gotten THE SCALE and there was not a lot of extra food to be had. She spent her time trying to play the piano and embroider and, as she explained, learning to become a lady. She wouldn't be excited for me in the least.

Finally, too tired to stay awake, I took my precious letter and put it under my pillow, touching it when I woke to be sure it was still there.

In the morning I didn't wake early and when I did, I didn't rush down to get the bread into the oven or the coffee made. Instead, I took the letter out and reread it for what must have been the tenth time. I casually filled the basin and washed my hands and face.

Edith was sent up to wake me and get me downstairs. I told her I would be down shortly.

When I got to the kitchen seven hungry faces stared at me from the table. It was hilarious to see them all following me with their eyes as I stoked the stove, got the bread ready to bake, ground the coffee and started a large pot to perk. I did not rush, nor did I explain. Finally Ethel could contain herself no longer.

"What has gotten into you? Are you sick or is this another one of your lazy days?" Of course her tone was sharp and sarcastic, and this morning I was not going to have it. I never had a lazy day. Not ever.

I turned around sharply. Striding to the table I slammed my hands down onto it with such force that everyone at it jumped and sat straight up.

Looking at Ethel I said in a stern voice, "Show me the contract."

Ethel's face went from red to white.

There was complete silence. They all seemed to be holding their breath.

"Don't you use that tone with me." She sounded equally stern, but not quite as firm as usual.

"Show me the contract," I repeated just as sternly as before.

"I don't have to show you anything. My word is good. There is a contract and that's all you have to know." The firmness was gone from voice.

"Show me the contract." I was not to be put off.

"Are you calling me a liar?" Her tone was testy and insulted. This was a very tricky reply. How would I answer?

"I am asking you to prove that you have a contract for my work here, a contract signed by the Whites."

"I don't know where it is. We have so much paperwork and you know how busy we are. I can't find it right now. Especially not on an empty stomach. Where is our breakfast?" Ethel was trying to turn this to her favor.

"Is that really why? Because your desk is untidy? Or it is because there is no contract?" Getting her to confess was not going to be easy.

"So why don't you just make our breakfast and you can come into the office later and we can find it together?" She was now working her way into her snake-oil tone I'd heard her use when she was trying to wheedle something out of someone.

"I will make your breakfast, but later you will all help with all of the chores around the inn. And I will see that contract when we're done with breakfast. Someone had better tend to the boarders' breakfasts, since I am such a lazybones." I cracked a dozen eggs into the frying pan and began scrambling.

"Edith, could you start some oatmeal for the boarders?" Ethel was syrupy as molasses.

Edith pumped some water into a kettle, set it on the stove to boil and went to the pantry for the oatmeal tin.

"I want Eunice to help too." I was going to milk this for all I could get.

"Mother, do I have to do as she says?" Eunice whined. "Really, this is insane."

"Eunice, it would be nice if you helped more around the inn." Ethel was gently trying to urge her firstborn into motion.

"I don't understand this. What is going on?" Eunice was about to have a tantrum.

"Eunice, get up and help," Ethel snapped.

Breakfast went quickly and the boarders were fed. Ethel rose to go upstairs.

"Mother," I said, trying not to sound sarcastic, "have you forgotten? You were going to look for the contract."

189

"Oh, oh, yes, give me a few minutes." She feigned forgetfulness and continued up the stairs.

I was beside myself. She could play with me for days, forgetting or mislaying or hiding papers. What could I do? I was at her mercy.

Then a most unanticipated occurrence restored my faith in humanity.

Chapter 38

That whole day Ethel avoided me. I was getting more help. Even the twins spent the morning in the garden weeding and picking squash and digging potatoes for our evening meal. They asked me what they could do and I showed them what were weeds and what were not and how to harvest vegetables. They proved to be fast and able learners and I wished I had had their help months ago. We could have made this lifesaving garden twice as large.

Everett, who was always willing to give a hand, fed and watered the chickens and brought in the eggs. Then he took his wagon to the store for some needed supplies. I was no longer using the scale. I decided to order what we needed on the inn's expense account. I didn't ask.

Edith had always been the most helpful around the inn so I sat with her at the table and did some of the mending, which made me wistful thinking of the days spent with Felicity.

Eunice was the most difficult. I'm sure Ethel gave her instructions to help out but she did it with reluctance and a moody countenance.

That afternoon Fitzy arrived, stomping up the granite steps to the inn, red in the face, looking sterner than I'd ever seen him.

"Millie, my girl." He opened the screen door and walked to the stove where I was stirring a pot of turnip porridge that was to be our supper along with several boiled chickens. He held me out at arm's length to look me over, then hugged me to his great chest.

"You look too thin. They aren't giving you enough to eat, are they?" He scowled. Then, so quickly I had trouble following his change of thought, he gave me a big grin. "So, my Millie is getting married?" I nodded and he smiled some more. "When do I get to meet the lucky fellow?"

"You already know him. Remember, you invited him to the ball. Johnny Knight, remember?"

"Oh yes! Johnny Knight. I knew he was smart. Isn't he a machinist?" I nodded again. Fitzy looked sad.

"The ball." He pulled out his handkerchief and passed his hand across his eyes, then blew his nose. "Those were wonderful days, weren't they? I sorely miss those days."

"I miss them too." He looked at me thoughtfully. I could imagine what he might be thinking but he didn't reveal it on his face or in his tone.

"Millie, I'm afraid we've done you a grave injustice and I am here to try to right it. Where are the elder Blacks?" He looked around the kitchen. Then in a quiet voice, leaning towards me, he said, "The place doesn't look like it did when we were running it, does it?" I shook my head.

"No. I try to keep it up but I have to do most of the work myself, and they are very tight with the funds so I have to do without. I often run out of soap, thread, flour, sugar, salt. We never have enough."

"I can see you look like you don't get nearly enough to eat. What are they doing with their money?" Fitzy was dumbfounded.

"I only know they don't pay me a cent and expect me to do more work than I did when you were running the place. They have more boarders too, of a sad class because the good clients left when the food and lodgings became so poor. We don't change the sheets but twice a month, and sometimes only once a month. I could tell you things you would not believe."

Fitzy looked thoughtful. "Some things I can't change. This is their inn now, and even if they run it into the ground there is nothing I can do. But I can see to it that you are not forced to work here another minute if you don't want to, and I can also see to it that they give you any back pay they might owe you. Have you any record of your employment hours?"

"No, but I can tell you that I work almost non-stop from five in the morning until ten at night. I break for quick meals, and some of them are taken on the hoof. I took a half day off last month to go on a picnic with Johnny and I bought the provisions from the money you gave me and didn't take anything from here. That is the only time off I've had since you left."

Fitzy almost looked like he would cry, but "I'm sorry, my dear" was all he said.

"I think Erastus is in the taproom, watering down the whiskey, and Ethel is upstairs. Shall I get her?"

"Yes, you get Ethel and I'll get Erastus."

As I went to find Ethel I pondered Fitzy's return. For a man not given to exposing his softer side, he seemed very contrite. It could only have been because I was engaged to

Johnny. Otherwise the cloud of Felicity's declaration would have hung over me, and it seemed to have dissipated.

Minutes later we all met in the kitchen. I brewed tea. Fitzy, whom the Blacks were surprised to see, began this meeting of the innkeepers with exaggerated politeness. "Well, how nice to see you both again." He started, "I'm sorry it's under such difficult circumstances." He motioned for the two of them to sit and they did. I poured tea for everyone and the Blacks stirred theirs nervously. Fitzy remained standing and slowly circled the table so they had to move their heads around and around to follow him.

"How has the inn been for you since we last met? Satisfactory? Has it been profitable?" This seemed to confound the Blacks, who would normally have complained about how poor business was and how they could barely scrape together two cents. Should they say that now or should they claim business has been fine? Watching the emotions cross their faces I could discern the working of their minds. Why was he here? If they knew why he had come today they would know how to approach him. I followed their eyes moving from Fitzy to each other and then back to Fitzy.

Erastus spoke first. "Well, business has fallen off, and we've had a hard time because expenses seem to keep rising."

Ethel nodded. "Yes, and someone had been pilfering food, so we were even forced to purchase a scale to keep from losing our inventory."

Fitzy stopped and faced her. "Pilfering food, you say? By the looks of you none of you are guilty." He chuckled at his own joke.

"Well, the scale helped with that." Ethel had to get her comment in.

"I see." Fitzy started to work towards his goal. "What about other expenses? Are they overburdening you?"

Erastus and Ethel again exchanged glances. "Well, we do use too much wood and coal. I wish we could cut back on that, but the windows let through so much cold air in the winter. Soap, too—we go through a lot of soap, which is very expensive." Ethel was ticking off the inventory in her mind. "Beef is expensive. We try to make it last." This almost made me choke. Her idea of making it last was to serve it as a paper-thin sliced roast, and any leftovers would be mixed with flour and water and served over bread in the morning, and leftovers from that would be made into soup, on and on until the remaining tasteless grey mass even the chickens wouldn't eat.

"I see." Fitzy pressed towards his goal. "What about your staff? Are they very costly? Have they demanded a higher salary?"

Suddenly Erastus and Ethel knew why he had come. The look they exchanged was priceless beyond measure.

"Why, no, they are not very costly." Erastus didn't know how to answer.

"Do you employ anyone other than Millie?" Fitzy was circling like a hawk.

"We all work here." Ethel went to her indignant tone.

I stared at her, shocked. Fitzy caught the look.

"All of you work at the inn?"

"Yes, but we all have different jobs. Erastus runs the taproom, I do the books, and Edith helps Millie with the dishes..." She couldn't fabricate quickly enough to cover her dishonesty.

"Yes, I see, and what do your other children do?"

Ethel was again indignant. "I don't see why this is any business of yours. I don't like being interrogated like this, as though we were common criminals. You sold the inn to us, we own it and we can do as we please." She stood up, ready to leave.

Fitzy pounced. "Sit down, Ethel." Ethel sat down. "I am here because my Millie has been laboring under some kind of what I will politely call misunderstanding. Did you tell her you had a contract signed by us for two years of employment?"

Ethel swallowed hard. "I guess it was a misunderstanding, as you say." She looked to Erastus for a helpful word, but got just the opposite.

"I told you we shouldn't have led her on like that. What were you thinking?" Erastus spoke under his breath but loudly enough that we could all hear it.

"We needed her to stay on. It's not illegal to mislead someone. We couldn't have run the inn without her." Ethel hoped that a businessman would understand.

"Well, what you have done is illegal. You didn't mislead her, you misrepresented the terms of her employment. And the worst part is you didn't even pay her. If you had, she would not likely have wanted to leave the only home she's ever known." Fitzy faced them as he leaned into his hands he had planted on the table. He was an intimidating presence. "So the question is now, what are you going to do to make it right?" He stood up and crossed his arms.

Chapter 39

The Blacks were beaten. Erastus put his head into his hands. Ethel looked panicked.

"I--I--I don't know what to do." Ethel looked close to tears. "We can't afford to pay her. I guess we can release her from the contract, though."

At this Fitzy blew up. "Contract?" he bellowed. "What contract? There is not and never has been a contract to release her from!" I'd rarely seen him in such a state. "You've imagined this for so long that you must believe it's true."

At this Ethel did cry, big heaving sobs. Erastus put his arm around her shoulder and looked reproachfully at Fitzy. Finally her tears subsided and she spoke. "We have no money to pay her. If we did we would. We would pay her."

Fitzy looked from them to me. "Is there a telephone in town?"

"Yes," I volunteered, "I think Wellwood's has one you can use. Or the town hall if they don't."

"Millie, set me up a room for tonight. I'm going to get to the bottom of this." I nodded, eyeing the Blacks. They looked horrified. Fitzy went out the door and strode purposefully down the walk towards the store.

The Blacks went into the office. I could hear talking, sometimes low and intense, sometimes with their voices raised, but I couldn't quite make out what it was they were saying.

Finally they emerged. Ethel went upstairs without even looking at me, and Erastus went towards the taproom. With a backward glance he hissed at me, "You've ruined everything."

I had no idea what was happening. I just continued setting up for supper, folding sheets in between stirring the porridge and laying the table.

I could hear heavy feet upstairs and the sound of furniture being moved. The whole afternoon was one of the strangest of my life. When Fitzy came back he asked to dine in the guests' dining room rather than at the table with us. He very formally gave Erastus payment for the night he was staying. I made sure to give him one of the most well-appointed rooms. This was not easy since most of our nicer furniture had disappeared and we had only second-rate dressers, beds and bedding and poor worn rag rugs. I couldn't remember things being moved out or broken, but I realized the inn wasn't furnished now the way it once had been.

I set Fitzy up in the dining room at a private table so I could serve him the choicest meal before the boarders had a chance to quickly help themselves to the best of the fare, leaving little or no treats for the slower, more refined guest. He bought a bottle of wine from Erastus that I served to him.

Fitzy went out after supper to visit, he said, some old friends he hadn't seen for months and was eager to catch up with. I gave him a key to the front door so he could come in at his convenience.

Rather than having all the help I wanted that evening, I had none. I had expected to get an overwhelming show of support from the now defeated Blacks. Instead my family rushed through their meal and deserted the table, disappearing into their rooms. Anyone else would have gotten suspicious, but not I, so full of innocence. I just imagined a new phase in their stewardship.

I did my evening chores, which took longer without help, kneaded the bread, ground the coffee and set the table. Then I sat at the table and uncharacteristically drank a glass of wine from the bottle Fitzy had bought, relaxing and thinking about the day. I finished off the last of the bottle and went up to our darkened bedroom with only a single small candle, not wanting to wake the two other girls already sound asleep.

I awoke late the next morning to an empty room. It would not have surprised me if Edith was up and downstairs already, but I couldn't imagine that Eunice would be up earlier than I was. When I went downstairs neither of them were in the kitchen. Nor did I find them in the guest dining room, the pantry, out with the chickens, or in the taproom. Finally I went back upstairs and checked Erastus and Ethel's room. It was empty too. Then I opened their dresser. Empty. I went back to my room to the girls' dressers. Empty. I went to the boys' room. They weren't there.

The Blacks were gone. Gone! I was aghast. I couldn't believe it.

I ran up to Fitzy's room and knocked.

Fitzy opened the door, and I told him what I'd found.

"I'm not surprised, my dear. Actually I expected it. You go down and start breakfast I'll be down shortly and tell you what I've found."

I obeyed, still unbelieving. I went around the inn kitchen, trying to see if things looked and felt the same. I started my morning: stoked the stove, put the coffee on and readied the bread. I wasn't sure how I felt about this. Mostly I was relieved. I didn't have that heavy presence hanging over me like a vulture watching my every move, waiting for me to slip. But where did they go and what would happen to the inn? What would happen to me?

Since the lodgings had become so sad we no longer had many boarders, so I splurged and instead of our regular egg toast or oatmeal I made a large batch of scrambled eggs and a few slices of bacon to go with the hot bread fresh from the oven. The boarders, upon my entrance to their dining room, looked greedily and gratefully at the offered fare. They thanked me more than once as I poured their coffee.

Fitzy came into the kitchen smiling, inhaling deeply the aroma of freshly baked bread. We sat down to eat and he started to explain.

"Millie, I'm afraid we've both been hoodwinked." He sipped his coffee, sampling it gently to ensure it wasn't too hot. "I visited my old attorney, who said we could bring a suit against them if they didn't agree to pay you. I thought that if we threatened them, they would." He took another sip of coffee as I brought him a plate of scrambled eggs, bacon and bread.

"Then I went to my banker, the one who handled the mortgage on the inn, and he said they were in arrears. They had made several early payments but in the last four months they paid nothing and the bank was about to ask them to leave or file for bankruptcy." He took a couple mouthfuls of eggs, slowly savoring them as he broke off a piece of bacon and laid it on the bread, and that too he savored. Wiping his moustache with his napkin, he changed the subject. "I thought you were almost starving, but this is a fine breakfast."

I was anxious to hear everything he had to say about the Blacks but I had to explain. "Yesterday when I confronted them about the contract I was so angry that I had the youngest Black go to the market and pick up whatever I thought we needed and put it on the inn's tab. I was not going to starve any longer." Fitzy smiled and scooped up another big forkful of eggs.

He continued. "I've been checking with the sheriff too. I think there must be some reason that no matter how much money they made they never had enough to cover their expenses. The sheriff said he would look into the matter." He cleaned his plate, wiping up egg with the last of the bread. Pushing back from the table he pulled out a cigar. "Would you mind awfully if just this once I had a cigar in the kitchen? Florence would never let me do it, but just this once?" He looked at me, eyebrows raised inquiringly.

"Okay, just this once." What else could I say?

"We've got a lot to talk about, you and I. What is going to happen now with the inn?" Fitzy of course was in touch with the reality that I had not even started to think about. Yes, what would happen to the inn?

"While I was out last night I stopped by Johnny's." He blew out smoke and watched my face, trying to gauge how I would respond. I was surprised but not upset. "Well, I invited him to supper. I expect him to come by around five, so perhaps you should get our supper going and put on your best dress." He smiled and hugged me again. Before I could ask him any questions he headed out the door, leaving me curious and unnerved.

I rushed around. I still had boiled chicken left from yesterday so I decided to make pot pies. I went outside to pick peas and pull carrots.

Chapter 40

I set the boarders' table, then our kitchen table, pulled three fine chicken pot pies from the oven and then ran upstairs to clean up and dress.

When I came down Fitzy was already in the kitchen, leaning over the pot pies.

I delivered two of the pies to the boarders with some cheese and bread and a pot of tea. Then I nervously fussed in the kitchen until I heard Johnny at the door. Fitzy greeted him and led him to the table as I brought the pot pie and set it down.

"Johnny, you're lucky to be getting such a fine cook for your wife." Johnny came around the table and kissed my cheek.

"I know," he said proudly. We sat down, Fitzy at the head and Johnny and I on each side. Fitzy served the still-warm supper and we enjoyed it with a glass of wine he'd hidden in his room.

"Well, Johnny, have you heard any rumors?"

"Yes, I heard something about the Blacks. Is it true? Did they leave town in a hurry?"

"So fast they couldn't take all the wine with them." Fitzy lifted his glass and chuckled.

"What happened?" Johnny was curious and I wondered if Fitzy knew more than he'd told me so far.

"Well, it seems they've defaulted on the mortgage and the bank was going to foreclose. We haven't sorted everything out yet. I need to see if there is anything interesting in the office. I was hoping to find something of value to give to Millie, who worked for them all these months without getting paid. She deserves a reward for all of that loyalty and hard work, don't you think?" Johnny nodded.

"But," Fitzy continued, "the question is, what is to become of the inn?" Johnny looked at me I looked at Fitzy. "Johnny, you've been working at Mason's for how many years now?"

"Twelve. I started apprenticing when I was eight, just doing little jobs, but I had the aptitude, they said, and I worked my way up."

"Twelve years." Fitzy fingered his moustache, "That's a long time to be working somewhere. You must have saved up some money in that time, living at home?" Fitzy was fishing.

"Yes, I have some savings." Johnny wasn't giving the information away. Fitzy would have to work for it.

"Would you say you had enough of a down payment for, say, an inn?" Fitzy was out with it.

"Oh, no, sir, not that much." Johnny shook his head.

"Would you say you had two thousand dollars?"

"Um, yes, almost that."

"I'd say then that you do have enough for a down payment, and what you don't have Millie will help you with. And I can loan you both enough to make some repairs and upgrades that we all know need to be made."

We both stared at him, shocked. What an idea! Johnny and I buying the inn! It was wonderfully frightening.

"Why not?" Fitzy went on. "Millie has been carrying this place for nineteen years at least. Wouldn't it be a fine thing if she could manage it too?" He took my hand and then Johnny's. "I think this place could be great again. I heard there were plans in the works to run a trolley up Main Street. Do you know what *that* would do for business?" He joined our hands across the table. "Of course, Johnny, you would have to be married before you could move in."

Johnny and I looked at each other. It was almost too much to take in. It sounded incredibly perfect, really too good to be true.

"I talked to the banker. He's an old friend of mine, and he agreed we could transfer the mortgage. But we can't dilly-dally, so you'll need to make up your minds soon."

I wanted to dance, to waltz around the room like a princess. I could never have imagined that not only would I be out from under those nasty people but I would own the roof over my head and be married to a fine man! I watched Johnny. Although he seemed interested I could tell the idea didn't thrill him the way it thrilled me.

Fitzy got up. "Well, I'll leave you two to discuss this. I know there's a lot to take in. Take your time, but hurry up." He chuckled.

Johnny looked at me intently. "Honestly, it scares me. All my life I have saved. I guess I didn't know what I was going to do with my savings, maybe invest in the cartridge factory, but this wasn't the first thing that came to mind."

I nodded. "I understand. We have time to think it over." I didn't want to put pressure on him.

"Now that the Blacks are gone and you're free from their tyranny, do we even need to rush into anything? I guess I thought you could live with me at my parents' house or we could board for a while until I could perhaps afford a house. I don't know if I was thinking that far ahead. Now that it's in front of me, I'm not sure what I want." He was scaring me.

"Do you still want to marry me?" I asked timidly. One minute I had been near ecstasy, and now it was so far away.

His expression was serious. "Yes, I think so."

Diana K. Perkins

Part 3

Diana K. Perkins

Chapter 41

Fitzy was out the next time Johnny came. We had a light supper together. The poorer boarders who had stayed on received soup and bread, their normal evening fare. Johnny sat across from me quietly, almost shyly. I was afraid. Afraid to ask what he thought about taking over the inn, afraid he might have changed his mind about marrying me. He didn't voice his thoughts, only remarking that it was strangely quiet in the kitchen without a big family bustling about.

"I haven't told my parents about it, about the inn. Maybe we could have them over one evening?"

"Okay, that sounds like a good idea. When? This week sometime?" I thought this could be the buildup to a serious move, maybe marriage, maybe talk of taking on the inn too. Perhaps he needed them to understand, to meet me, to like me. Surely he didn't need their permission. He was old enough to make decisions for himself.

"Yes, maybe Sunday?" It was Wednesday, so he wasn't dragging his feet that much.

"Shall we invite Fitzy?" It made sense to me to invite the person who was as close to a parent as I could get.

"Yes, that's a good idea. I'll see you Sunday."

"You don't want to come by for supper before then?" I tried not to sound desperate. I wasn't accustomed to eating alone. I wasn't accustomed to doing anything alone.

"You'll be okay. Fitzy will be here." I couldn't read him. I had no idea what was going through his mind, but he didn't seem excited about any of the prospects before him. He kissed me and left. I made myself some tea.

My tea got cold as I daydreamed, relishing all the wonderful possibilities. We could marry, have a houseful of children, and run the inn. I would have lots of little hands to help, and would be sure none of them were spoiled and they all carried their load. I imagined I could be happy here with Johnny. Then like a flash Edith's question came back to me. "Do you love him?"

Must I love him to have a good life here with him? I knew there were people who lived long lives with someone they didn't love but they were satisfied, they were happy enough. They probably even fell in love after spending a lifetime together.

What would my future be? When the Blacks were here all I could think about was escaping the daily toil and deprivation. Johnny was my key to that escape. But now I didn't have the same need for a key. I needed one in a different way. I could not survive on my own. I wasn't sure I could get a job at a mill or if I could earn enough to be independent and perhaps board somewhere.

I was burdened with a different problem. What would I do? As I thought about it I was automatically going through the motions of washing the dishes, picking up the boarders' plates, cleaning, straightening, washing, drying. All the familiar motions gave me comfort.

Finally Fitzy came home. I told him what had transpired. He said it was a common experience that men went through before they married. They feared losing their independence and taking on responsibilities. Even he himself had experienced it before his marriage to Flo, which, he said, was the wisest choice he'd ever made.

"I'll talk to him," he reassured me. "Don't you worry anymore." And I trusted him to do it. He would make Johnny see the many benefits of marrying me and putting a down payment on the inn.

I slept fitfully that night, with so much to think about and no one else in the room. I wasn't accustomed to sleeping alone, to being aware of a dog barking in the night or a horse clomping by. I got up and looked for the letter from Felicity. I'd stored it in a small sachet bag in my drawer. I opened it and as it crinkled I thought I could smell her, I thought I could hear her whisper in the quiet of the night. And I remembered my little mouse, pressing me up against the summer ice. I knew passion. I knew love. It wasn't the same with Johnny. But I had to put Felicity behind me. Of all my choices a future with Felicity was the most impossible and thinking of it would only torment me. I put the letter under my pillow and considered destroying it before I became obsessed. I'd heard about women who became obsessed. They went mad and were put into homes. They called them homes but they really were hospitals for insane people.

I thought I could hear Fitzy snoring down the hall. It brought me back to my senses and the rhythmic sound finally lulled me to sleep.

Chapter 42

Fitzy was up before me. In the kitchen I could smell the stale scent of a cigar but he wasn't there. I went about making breakfasts and was very grateful there were so few people to care for. That meant not only smaller meals but fewer chamber pots and towels and sheets to do all by myself. Goodness, if we did get the place how would I manage if we actually had the inn even half full?

Fitzy came in whistling, a newspaper under his arm, and I served up scrambled eggs and fresh warm bread as he pulled out his chair. When I sat down he cleared his throat. "Well, I understand we'll be having supper with Johnny and his parents on Sunday." He gave me a knowing look, then turned to his breakfast.

"You've been to his house?"

"No, I went by the Mason's factory. Caught him just before he started work. Do you want to know what we talked about?"

"How did you have time to talk about anything? Didn't he have to go to work?" I was feeling anxious about this meeting between them. I thought we should just allow things to unfold as they would and not prompt them.

"Well, of course we talked about you, and about the inn, but also about his parents. I've been getting the feeling he doesn't want to leave home. He confirmed it, but not directly." I nodded, waiting to see if there was more.

"So, we'll see what happens on Sunday, but perhaps,"–he paused–"perhaps there is a way we can resolve this." I was concerned that his resolution might include Johnny's parents. I almost knew that was what he was thinking. I'd never met Johnny's parents. He didn't speak of them very often, but I got the feeling they had quite a bit of influence over him. Nothing definite was ever said, but he seemed quite concerned about what they thought. He told me they were watching over his savings and they wouldn't want him to be careless with his funds. This made me wonder if he was giving them his pay and he didn't have spending money or couldn't use his money as he wished. All of this flashed through my mind before I spoke.

"Really? Do you think you have a solution?"

"Well, my dear, we'll see on Sunday, won't we?"

"Do you think he really loves me and wants to marry me?" I'm not sure why I revealed my thoughts in such a personal question to Fitzy, but I needed to know and had no other confidant.

"Funny you should ask that." Fitzy paused to wipe his mouth. "I think he is very interested in you. He said he's been waiting patiently for almost two years, when we lived here and while the Blacks did. So I'd say he's very interested."

That relieved me. At least he had told Fitzy something that rang true, not that he'd ever been dishonest but he was always very quiet about his interest in me. He'd stop in, have tea, and perhaps brush my cheek on his way out. The closest he ever came to desire was that day on the picnic.

For him it was either very quiet interest or overbearing passion. Perhaps it made a difference that we didn't have the opportunity to go for walks hand-in-hand like other couples, or go out for a paddle on the lake, or steal a kiss in the root cellar. We'll see, as Fitzy said, we'll see. I was very eager for the weekend supper.

While we waited for our Sunday with the Knights, Fitzy made the rounds of the sheriff, the bank, and town officials. He came in one evening with news he was just bristling to share. He went to the taproom, which he had restocked with a keg and some basic liquors, and returned to the kitchen bringing a bottle and several glasses.

"Sit down, Millie, my dear. I've got some news for you." I was nervous that he'd seen Johnny again but he assuaged my fears almost immediately.

He poured a small amount of brandy for each of us.

"As you know, I've been spending some time with the sheriff. He has given me news about the Blacks. They were last in New York State, running confidence schemes. They've apparently been moving from state to state, presenting themselves as entrepreneurs to banks that sell them a property which they run into debt and strip of any assets before they skip town just in time to avoid being caught." He drank his brandy in one swallow, put the glass down hard and poured himself another.

"Sheriff Mulroy seems to think they are in Massachusetts now and he's alerted several banks hoping they'll be trying to find another business to purchase."

I was not too surprised but again felt assaulted by that nasty family, who had inflicted emotional wounds from which I was just beginning to recover.

It was my turn to reveal what seemed like their unlimited craftiness. "I still don't know how they managed to get some of the nicer furniture pieces out from upstairs. I never heard things move and didn't notice it missing until it was gone, but Ethel always answered my question with a simple declaration that they needed the money more than the furniture. I was in such a vulnerable position I couldn't argue. Now I realize that the wagon full of furniture was likely stolen from us and other poor trusting souls."

Fitzy shook his head angrily. "What scoundrels!" He polished off another brandy and poured a third. His face was red and he was snorting like a bull.

"I've got supper to serve to the boarders." I couldn't let my responsibilities slip. Fitzy watched me appraisingly.

"Why didn't my other girls turn out like you?" He said no more before he went outside and lit a cigar.

Chapter 43

The week seemed to drag, but every day I was gaining more confidence in my inn-keeping.

Boarders were responding to the quality of the food by bringing me little gifts, often of fresh food, thereby allowing me to serve larger quantities than they had ever before enjoyed under the Blacks' management. I began to think about trading services with a couple of them who seemed neater and more responsible. Perhaps they would help with the garden or mow the lawn, which had gone to high weed, or maybe paint a room, or repair furniture. The idea of being a proprietress was exciting. I'd been doing the hard work for years. I knew what was required, so why couldn't I take over the management too?

As Sunday drew closer I was even considering asking Fitzy to allow me to run the inn with or without Johnny. The more I thought about it, the faster the time seemed to pass. Now I wanted it to slow down so I would have more time to think about how I could approach the subject with both of them.

It was all taken out of my hands on Sunday. Fitzy had come into some money.

He'd taken care of the inn's balance at the store so I was able to order a turkey and extra staples to make a sumptuous feast and have some left for the inn.

When Sunday came I was ready. It wasn't too much different than my normal Sunday supper except it meant more to me than any other meal I ever prepared.

I'd told the boarders they'd have an early supper so afterward we could eat in the dining room with as much privacy as possible.

I was grateful the Blacks hadn't stolen the linens or most of the silver, although some of the larger serving pieces were missing. I imagined that rushing to take china in a wagon would only leave a box of smashed pieces, and the Blacks probably thought of that too. Fitzy's arrival must have spurred their decision to escape. When no one was watching they were likely squirreling away goods out on their wagon, which had been stored in the barn. Perhaps they just didn't have time to pack up the linens and silver.

The table was set, the candles lit, and a bouquet of roses from our bush topped off the elegance. Fitzy was wandering about nervously, straightening napkins and finally going to the taproom and pulling out a bottle of wine and another of brandy, from which he poured himself a glass.

I heard a commotion from the road and someone scream. I ran to the door and found Mr. and Mrs. Knight climbing the steps, both looking quite disturbed. Mrs. Knight paused to brush at her dress, which looked as though it was spattered with mud. As they came up the walk I stepped forward to welcome them.

"You must be Johnny's parents." I put my hand out and then saw Johnny coming up the steps behind them.

Mr. Knight turned towards the road. "Did you see that? Some idiot came charging down the road, lost control of his buggy and almost ran us over."

"I'm sorry, I didn't see it. Are you okay?"

"I will be once we're safely in the house. We live up on Wall Street. We don't usually get this crazy kind of traffic."

I stepped back to let them through, showing them into the front entryway. "Please come in and get comfortable." I directed them towards the dining room. Johnny followed, not brushing my cheek as he usually did but addressing me formally. "Hello, Millie. Thank you for inviting us." I felt this was a very strange start to the evening.

Fitzy came out of the kitchen carrying the bottle of wine and introduced himself as my father. His always cordial manner seemed to set people at ease.

As Fitzy poured the wine and chatted, I retrieved a towel for Mrs. Knight to wipe her dress.

"Thank you, dear. It's only mud and should brush off once it's dry." She seemed kinder than I had expected.

I began serving, first soup, then the turkey with the vegetable sides, and finally a superb blueberry pie. The wine and the food relaxed everyone. Fitzy brought out a second bottle.

Fitzy was not rushing the evening, probably hoping that Johnny would be the first to raise the subject of marriage. Finally he told Mr. Knight and Johnny to follow him into the taproom if they wanted a cigar. He rose and they followed. I was a little lost. I started to clear the table just to have something to do. Mrs. Knight stood up to help.

"You don't have to help me. You're our guest."

"Oh, pshaw, I do this every day." As we worked we started to talk about the inn. She asked about the Blacks, having heard the news about them. She asked what we were planning to do now that they were gone. I told her honestly that I didn't know. I could feel her watching me carefully, appraising me. I was conscious of every move I made, every word I spoke, every hair that fell into my face. Was I good enough? Was I suitable for her son?

Finally she approached the subject I was waiting for. "Johnny's not much of a talker. You've probably noticed that already." I pumped some water for tea.

"Yes, I have."

"But he's a good boy, and he speaks highly of you." I gave her a sideways glance and found her looking directly at me. She smiled. "I'm glad."

I was taken aback by her straightforward manner. I had expected to dislike her, but instead felt she was much nicer than I had thought she would be. Why on earth had I formed that impression in the first place? She was rather plain, not really pretty, but in her features I could see the resemblance to her son, and when she smiled she looked like another person. When she smiled she did look pretty.

"I guess you two are getting serious..." She was helping me carry the teapot and cream into the dining room. She continued, "...since he's never introduced us to another girl." She watched me intently. I was praying she wouldn't ask me if I loved him.

"Yes, I would say we're pretty serious. He's been very patient. I have very little time for courting and he's been willing to visit late or take a little time here and there when I can get it."

"Are you sure you've spent enough time together?" That was a fair question.

"Well, we haven't rushed into anything." And we both chuckled at that.

After that we sat and had tea and talked about Mr. Knight's job and about how Johnny and he went hunting and fishing together. When I mentioned that Johnny had given me two cartridges she stopped talking and looked hard at me. She told me Johnny hunted rabbits in his youth and brought them home for stew, and Orin would give him two cartridges, telling him to think of the creatures with respect and make a clean kill and to keep the cartridges for good luck. She said they were special to him. Then our conversation shifted to the inn and no longer focused on Johnny. I felt as though she'd gotten her questions answered and any further discussion wouldn't be productive. I was relieved.

Johnny, his father and Fitzy finally emerged from the taproom, all of them beaming.

"Well, my dear," Mr. Knight said, reaching for his wife's hand, "don't you think it's time for us to be off?" She rose, nodded to us, put on her shawl and allowed her husband to usher her out. Johnny followed. This time he did kiss me on the cheek and pressed the second of the cartridges into my hand.

It was all so abrupt I couldn't understand if it was a good sign or not.

Fitzy walked them to the door, full of good cheer and goodnights, and waved them off.

He sat down at the table and poured himself a cup of tea. "A very nice evening, wouldn't you say?" I nodded. "I like Mr. Knight very much and it was good to talk with Johnny too, since I haven't had much of a chance before this." He sipped his tea. "Oh, you've cleared all of the dishes. Were we gone that long?"

"Yes, you were gone an hour easily." I could tell he was playing with me, knowing I wanted to hear what was discussed and what the outcome was.

He stood up. "Well, I'm tired and am off to bed."

"Oh no you're not!" I surprised myself. "You will tell me what you talked about or I won't let you sleep a wink."

Fitzy laughed.

Chapter 44

Fitzy sat down at the kitchen table and again poured a little brandy into our glasses.

"Well, my dear, I think we'll be keeping the inn." He paused to take a sip. I watched him, wanting him to come out with it, but he was savoring his brandy and was going to take his time.

"So, so, so?"

"What do you want, Millie?" He looked hard at me. "Are you sure you want to marry this fellow?" He didn't wait for me to reply. "Because if you do, I believe he is the perfect match. He seems like a decent fellow, hardworking, respectable, and I like his father." I nodded. "Did you get to talk to his mother? Do you like her?"

"Yes, I liked her more than I thought I would." He looked somewhat surprised at that.

"Well, we haven't worked out all the details, but I think that if you marry him and you think you can get more of our guests back, we should be able to keep the inn."

"That was what I was hoping."

"You were hoping to marry, or to keep the inn?"

"Both. But how will we manage? Have you talked to the bank? It's in default, right?"

"Yes, the Blacks stopped paying and the bank was going to put it up for auction, but I worked it out with them and they will let us have it for a certain amount over the auction starting bid."

"But where are you getting the money?"

"Well, Millie, do you remember when we had to leave and we went to Springfield to stay with Flo's mother?" I nodded. "Her mother passed away a couple months ago and left us quite a comfortable sum. I've invested some of it, but we agreed that if we could, we'd use the rest to get the inn back up."

"Gee, that's wonderful. But you will still own it, right?"

"Well, we'll own it for a while. We thought we might try to hold the mortgage while you pay it off so that eventually it would be yours. Yours and Johnny's."

I couldn't believe it. I was going to be an innkeeper! I would work for myself! It was too incredible to comprehend.

I got up and hugged Fitzy.

"Oh. Oh, stop." He hugged me back for a second then pushed me away. "Don't think it will be easy. You may be doing more work than you ever have. And maybe if you're lucky, you'll get some extra help in a year or two." He winked and chuckled to himself.

"Will you be staying in Springfield?"

"Yes, we're comfortably situated there. We have a number of acquaintances, and Flo seems to like the city life and not having the morning-to-evening work she had here." He drained his brandy glass. "Frankly I can't understand why you would want to keep working here when you could just have a nice little home with Johnny, instead of this thirty-room monstrosity."

"I know you don't mean that. You loved running this place."

He nodded. "Yes, but I didn't do that much of the work."

"So, what's next?" I was hoping to get more from him before he went to bed.

"I guess we'll have to set a date for, you know, the wedding." He smiled at me. "That's what you were hoping to hear, wasn't it?" I nodded.

"Just so that you know," he added, "I asked the Knights if they wanted to stay here and help you, but Orin said they didn't think they wanted to. They said they'd help if you needed it, but it would be better to leave you two alone. He said something about having his in-laws hanging too close when they first got married.

"Well, I'm going up. It's been a long day and I know you've got plenty to do tomorrow." He rose and I hugged him again.

"Thank you, Father. This is wonderful, more that I could ever have imagined. So much to do, so much to think about." He smiled and went up the stairs.

I sat at the table, finishing my brandy. Then I started the bread for the next morning.

Chapter 45

Another night of little sleep, but tonight it was from excitement. I could hardly believe my good luck! I felt overjoyed. But before I could finish savoring my good fortune, I felt guilty, as though I didn't deserve it. Then I felt a sense of doom. Nothing this good ever came my way, and something really terrible was probably going to happen to offset it.

Johnny was a nice boy, his mother was nice, and although I hadn't spent much time with his father he seemed nice too. Did I deserve this? Would I disgrace these nice people? I hoped it was because I was unaccustomed to such treatment, to such goodness, that I felt this way. Why wouldn't I deserve to be treated kindly and generously? Why not? I was no better or worse that the average person on the street, and none of them seemed to be weighed down with feelings of inadequacy.

Then I started to think about how I would manage the inn on my own. Would I, would we, struggle? Could we afford it? Would I need help?

Those questions would be resolved in a couple of weeks in a most unexpected way.

As I took upon myself more of the management of the inn, I found it difficult to justify feeding such hearty meals to those boarders who shared rooms. In at least one case they slept three to a room splitting the same price a single occupant would have paid. When we were scrimping and giving them poor meals I didn't think our rates unfair, but I saw the need to raise their rate when they were getting fine breakfasts and suppers but bearing no share of the cost increase.

So at supper the next evening I proposed a modest rate increase, even offering them single rooms for a reasonable fee since in the near future we would allow no more than two boarders to a room and at the higher rate. I tried to help them realize they would be more comfortable. Most of the fellows were not too upset about the plan, admitting that not only was the food now better and more plentiful but the sheets were changed more often and other amenities had improved. So only a small amount of grumbling accompanied my first step towards making the inn self-supporting. Dessert that night, a very nice pie with ice cream that two of the boarders who helped in the kitchen had cranked out, made the change more palatable.

Although most boarders were already in back rooms I started moving the rest of them to the quieter parts of the inn where I knew their comings and goings wouldn't disturb the other guests.

Johnny and I set our wedding date for spring the next year. Johnny started coming by after work and helping with some of the heavier chores, heading home after supper.

Fitzy was satisfied that everything had settled down and the inn was running smoothly. He knew if I needed any help I could call on Johnny or his parents, who had offered to step in if I asked. So he went back to Springfield, where

I'm sure he was missed since in his absence letters from Springfield were arriving frequently.

Not long after he left he wrote to say he would be returning in three weeks with very exciting news. I tried to imagine what could be so exciting. Perhaps Foster had come home?

I was shocked late one evening when a racket in the yard drew me out to find Fitzy driving up to the inn in an automobile! Apparently an investment of his in the Packard auto line had produced what he called "a good return."

But that wasn't the excitement he'd referred to.

Coventry was installing a water system in the village area! It would be gravity-fed from the lake, and water would be piped into the inn!

I couldn't imagine it. Water at my fingertips! And Fitzy planned to put in a flush toilet, a sink and a bathtub on each floor of the inn! The luxury this offered our customers was beyond imagination. It was also a lifesaver for me since more guests were returning to our establishment. I wouldn't be required to empty chamber pots, or bring ewers of water to the rooms and clean out the basins. I would have water at the kitchen sink without having to pump it. It was so exciting to me and to everyone who visited. We were getting electricity too. We were now going to be a first-class destination.

To top it all off Fitzy had a telephone installed in the office. I was afraid all these improvements would cause a flurry of business that I wasn't prepared for, and I wasn't entirely wrong.

Although the improvements didn't happen right away, I tried to prepare. I saved money and put it into the bank in an attempt to get every little bit I could, not for my wedding but for improvements to the inn. I hoped to gradually purchase new linens and rugs and little things that would appeal to the higher-paying weekend and day guests.

As fall approached and installation of the plumbing commenced, the regular cleaning and sanitary activities didn't change. The new bathing rooms were to be the first-floor linen closet, Fern's old room, and a room on the third floor, all of which were now thrown into disarray. While my kitchen pump was out of use for two days during installation of a faucet, one of the boys kindly brought in buckets from the well. I returned the favor with cookies and tea.

The fellows who were boarding knew my history at the hands of the Blacks and had also experienced their poor treatment, and they were more than willing to help me now that our fortunes had changed. Only one of them left our inn to live at a cheaper factory boarding house.

Johnny proved to be a respectable handyman, taking care of some needed carpentry and maintenance work. He even bought a used icebox for the kitchen. No longer did I have to run out to the root cellar to store food that would otherwise spoil.

I had expected to have more free time without the need to empty chamber pots and basins, but for some reason found that I didn't. With several more boarders coming on my cooking duties seemed doubled.

Much-needed help came unexpectedly.

Chapter 46

One evening after Johnny had gone home and I was finishing up the kitchen chores and steeping some tea, a soft knock at the kitchen door startled me.

In a flash fearsome thoughts raced through my mind. Who would be knocking at our door at this time of night? Johnny might knock gently but then he'd come in. Fitzy would have written or even called before coming. The boys would use the back door, and guests at the front door would ring from the office. Even Felicity came to mind with a pang. So much flashed through my mind in those few seconds it took me to cross the kitchen and open the door.

There on the doorstep, looking bedraggled and worn, stood Edith, clutching a sack to her chest. She gave me a pathetically sad look.

"I'm so sorry," she heaved out before she dropped the sack and grabbed my hand.

I was so dumbstruck it took a few seconds before I recognized her, picked up her sack and pulled her into the kitchen. She was dirty and seemed even weaker and thinner than she had been while she lived here with the miserly Blacks.

"Sit down. Let me get you some tea." I pushed her towards a chair at the table. I busied myself pouring her tea and slicing some of the day's leftover bread, which I served to her with butter and jam.

I could see she wanted to talk but instead she ravenously devoured the bread and tea, clutching the cup as though it was her lifeline to warmth and comfort. I watched as the color slowly came back into her cheeks. Finally she slowed her pace of bread consumption, finished the tea and began to speak while I refilled her cup.

"I'm so sorry, I'm so sorry," she sobbed as tears filled her eyes. I reached across the table and held her hand.

"I hated what we did to you. I felt so guilty, but I couldn't tell you or do anything but go along with them."

"Well, your family treated me badly, but thankfully things have turned out well for me. My father stepped in to save the inn and I am to be married in the spring. But what happened to you? Why are you here?"

"I ran away and it has taken me weeks to get here. At night I hid in barns, and sometimes kind people would give me rides in farm wagons." I looked down at her shoes, which were worn beyond repair and had what looked like newspaper poking out in spots.

"You must have walked much of the way." She nodded and another tear ran down her cheek.

I couldn't help but feel sorry for her. I took some of the leftover roast from the icebox, sliced off several pieces and offered them to her. She hesitated, giving me such a pathetic look that I had to encourage her.

"Aren't you still hungry? It's okay. Here, have some. We have plenty." I pushed the plate closer to her. She picked up the fork and knife and cut off little pieces that she chewed with a grimace, explaining, "My mother hit me and broke a tooth. It still hurts." I could only shake my head.

Gradually she started to feel better and snippets of the story came out. I tried to encourage her.

"You can tell me what happened. I don't resent you. You were always good to me." This brought tears to her eyes once again.

"We, my family that is, had been playing bad tricks on people. Bad tricks on gullible people, as if their innocence were their failing. At least that was how my mother explained it to us, but she made us believe we had to keep at it to live and if we didn't go along with her the police would catch us and put us in jail."

I nodded. "Yes, the jail part is probably true."

"So, we had done this at other places, gone in, taken over the business, stolen and sold everything and run off with whatever money we could. I didn't really know that much of what we were doing except for thieving goods. I didn't know the rest until we came here and I saw how conniving we were and how we left your inn with such a debt. But Mother was trying to indoctrinate me into the 'family business' as she would call it and I couldn't stomach it any longer. It was then, the night we ran out on you that she hit me with a candlestick and knocked me out. The next thing I remember I was on the wagon with a pain in my head and a broken tooth and no glasses. I didn't even know where we were, but we had left the town behind. We all had our bags packed and things in the wagon before supper. We went to bed in our clothes so all we had to do was steal out and harness the horses. We were very quiet and purposely tried to be sure we wouldn't wake you or Fitzy. We escaped unnoticed; no light went on. We were on our way hours before dawn, following back roads to avoid notice." She paused to sip her tea.

"We were heading for Massachusetts, where my father had seen an advertisement for an establishment that was going onto the auction block. I don't know how close we were to our destination, but I know we were in Massachusetts when one night I was able to steal away. I couldn't take much with me but I ran and ran and when I couldn't run anymore I found a bridge to sleep under. I tried to avoid most people because I thought I might look suspicious. I'd been on the road for several days, sleeping wherever I could and stealing eggs from chicken coops when I needed food and sucking them out, raw. I became so tired and weak I didn't care if people saw me and sometimes a farmer would stop and pick me up and take me for a few miles. I knew I wanted to come back here, hoping somehow I could make things right, hoping somehow the inn hadn't been sold again. Gradually I was able to find my way back. I'm grateful that it's night since some of the people in town might recognize me and would probably not be thinking very highly of me." She paused again to sip.

"Well, that's quite a story." I poured more tea for myself and for her.

"It's true, every word of it."

"I believe you."

"Can I stay here tonight?" I was surprised at her directness. "I can help you. I can wash the linens, cook and clean, empty chamber pots. I can do whatever you need. You know I'm a good worker." She was pleading.

"Well, you can certainly stay here tonight. I can't make this decision by myself, but I will tell Johnny and Fitzy how much I respect you for coming back and being honest and how you've never been afraid to work."

She visibly sagged, put her head in her hands and wept silently. I patted her on the shoulder.

"There, there, don't worry. I think they will agree that I need another person and you will probably be perfect." I stood up and she picked up her sack to follow me.

"What's in the sack?" I was curious as to what, in her desperation, she would have chosen to, take with her. She looked guilty.

"Things that belong here... a library book from the library here that I was hoping to bring back. I'm afraid the late fees will be more than I can afford."

"Don't worry. We'll explain it to them, and I'm sure they will be happy just to have the book back." I couldn't help but compare her to Fern, who found books so dear.

"Come on now, why don't you get cleaned up? You'll be happy to know there are no more chamber pots to empty and we have bathtubs in the house with hot water."

She got up, picked up her sack and followed me upstairs to my room. She reached into the sack and laid the book on the second bed where I had indicated she could sleep. I'd moved back to my old bedroom after the Blacks left, the room I had shared with Felicity. The book, *The Yellow Wallpaper*, was only slightly worn. I went to the bathroom across the hall and started to draw her a bath. "You will feel so much better once you've had a warm bath." When I came back I watched as she reached into the bottom of the sack and drew out another object and placed it carefully upon the bed. The scale. The damned scale had come back to our house.

"Heavens!" I exclaimed when she put it down.

"I thought you should be the one to have the last say on the scale." She eyed me fearfully, trying to gauge my reaction. After the surprise of seeing the cursed object I began to see the humor in it and started to laugh. I laughed long enough for Edith to appreciate the absurdity of it and then we both laughed together.

While she was bathing I looked through the trunk of old clothes left behind by the Whites for shoes and clothes that would fit her.

This may be, I thought, the most fortunate happening since Fitzy saved the inn.

Chapter 47

I awoke the next morning remembering all the events of the previous evening. I looked across to Edith's bed. She was sound asleep. I rose quietly, dressed, and went downstairs to start breakfast.

I had left a change of clothes for her at the end of her bed, knowing they might be somewhat too large but at least they were clean.

As I was scrambling up a large skillet of eggs Edith came down wearing the clothes I'd left out for her, carrying her tattered ones rolled up in a ball.

"Shall I put these in the laundry?"

"Yes, of course. I'm glad you found that dress I left for you. And the shoes--how do they fit?" She looked down at her feet. The shoes were a little large so she shuffled, but still they were better than what she'd been wearing. The dress hung off her like skin off a skeleton.

"The shoes will be fine, thank you." She smoothed the wrinkles on the dress and without any prompting went to the pantry and retrieved an apron, then stood by the table as though to start working. "What can I do?" I felt sorry for her. I knew she was desperate.

"You can slice up some bread. The toaster is on the shelf. Toast half a dozen slices on the stove. Have you done that before?" She nodded. "Then put the butter on the boarders' tables, and pour some milk into the pitcher and put that on their table too."

She went right to work. She was efficient, smart and quick. I was hoping Fitzy and Johnny would see their way to letting her stay, and I thought if she was here helping me before they found out by it might be to her advantage.

Once she'd finished those chores I asked her to bring in a block of ice, rinse the sawdust off and replace the diminishing block that was in the icebox. This was a somewhat dirty job since the pan under the icebox needed to be emptied and often it spilled, so then the floor had to be mopped. The blocks were heavy, and I hoped it wasn't too much for someone who had grown so thin, but she seemed to manage without complaint. I put her to some of the less savory and tedious tasks, all of which she approached with thoughtfulness and vigor. All day she worked. I was surprised how someone so haggard could keep going for so long, but it was quite possible she was now getting more to eat than ever before in her life. She'd had a healthy breakfast and also at mid-morning we had toast and tea, and at dinner we made slices of the roast into sandwiches.

We cooked several chickens for supper and with her help I made a very nice dessert. In my mind the test would be when Johnny arrived for supper. I planned to have her working upstairs when he came so I could ease him into her arrival and cushion the shock of seeing her.

My plan worked. She was upstairs when he arrived and I sat with him for a little tea before supper. I told him how she had showed up at the door. He of course was surprised. Then I told him she had apologized and helped me all day, and that she had been coerced into working with her family but hated it and finally escaped and wanted to stay at the inn and help me. He was shaking his head. I could see his reception was not as understanding as mine. I told him how much she had helped me already that day and how much of a help she would be in the future and that I wanted to give her a try. He was still shaking his head. I almost begged, "Please, just give her a try. If she doesn't work out we can tell her to move on, but we could give her a try." He could see how much I wanted to have her stay. "Okay, but only for a week, and at the end of the week we can decide. Then if it works out we can check each week to see if she continues to be satisfactory. If not…"

"Thank you. I understand it is a trial, but I don't think we will be disappointed."

I was grateful all this transpired before she returned to the kitchen.

Johnny helped serve the boarders' meals and was picking up a large bowl of potatoes when Edith came down. She stopped in the doorway when she saw him.

"Johnny, you remember Edith, right?" I could see his hesitation. "She's going to help us out for a while, right, Edith?" She stepped into the room and eyed him warily.

"Yes, I remember her." He stood there with the bowl in his hand.

"You're going to be helping me for a while, aren't you, Edith?" I repeated, and she nodded.

"Yes, ma'am." She looked down.

"Don't be silly, Edith. You don't need to call me ma'am. Come on, help us set up the boarders' supper." I picked up the platter of chicken and held it out to her. She took it and followed Johnny into the dining room. When they returned we brought food to our own table and sat down.

We ate silently for a little while, and then Johnny, usually quiet, spoke. "So, Edith, what have you been doing since you left us in such a hurry?" She looked at him with dread, then stared down at her food. Moments passed, perhaps even a minute, and I could see tears dripping onto her plate.

"Johnny, I told you she did not want to be part of the scheme. Edith, tell him what happened." I was hoping hearing the story from her would soften his animosity towards her.

"I, I...," she stuttered, "I knew about their plan that night, but not until just hours before they did it. When I rebelled my mother hit me and broke my tooth." She pulled on the corner of her lip to show the broken tooth. "Then my brothers threw me into the back of the wagon. I didn't wake up until we were well out of town. Maybe a week went by on our journey north, maybe two, then one night when everyone was asleep, I saw my chance to get away and I ran. I figured that once I got a good start they wouldn't come after me. They were trying to escape in the other direction." She stopped and took a sip of milk. Johnny, who had been listening closely, nodded and motioned for her to continue.

"I slept in barns, trying to avoid being seen on the roads because I thought I might look suspicious. Finally after almost three weeks I arrived here. It was the place that I had liked the best. I liked Millie. As poorly as we treated her, she was still kind to me." She turned to me and apologized again.

Johnny's eyes went from her to me. "Well, let's see how this works out. You know I will be watching you. I'll tell the sheriff. He will want to talk to you. I hope that's okay?"

"Yes, I will talk to him. I know you'll be watching and I will make you glad I'm here. I promise." Now her tone was firmer. I hoped this appeased Johnny.

We finished our meal and Edith served the handsome deep dish apple pie. When we were done she helped collect the dishes from the boarders' table and ours. She and I washed and dried them while Johnny sat reading the paper, a habit I think he had picked up from Fitzy. Finally he went home and Edith and I had our evening tea. The day had gone as well as I could have hoped.

But who knew what the future would hold?

Chapter 48

With the upgrades and the addition of Edith the inn was beginning to feel like not only a first-rate establishment but even more like a home. The boarders were becoming more polite and they dressed more neatly for supper and even helped with some of the simpler chores. The inn was running more smoothly than I could ever remember. We were noticing that guests were coming just for supper, which was not common in the past, and we started to require reservations so we would be prepared for the extra mouths.

But our summer guests hadn't arrived yet and I knew that would be the challenge. Although people came for Christmas when they wanted to visit relatives or use us as a half-way stop on a long journey, the inn was not the bustling place it had once been. I hoped that when summer came around we would be ready, and word would have gotten out that we were the place to stay.

As the winter went by I was grateful for Johnny's assistance clearing the stairs and walkways of snow and carrying in large piles of wood to keep our fires burning. He ordered coal for the furnace, which he stoked in the evening. One of our boys, as I had begun to call them, would put in a dozen shovelfuls in the morning that would keep us until he returned in the evening.

Edith had, as she promised, become a reliable asset to our staff. With the plentiful food we offered she lost her skeletal look, and in fact grew rather attractive. Even Johnny seemed to become accustomed to her, and our meals were full of pleasant talk about the inn, the factory and any local news we'd heard.

Edith and I began planning the wedding. Johnny was happy to have any thought of it taken off of his hands. Since it was a few months away we had plenty of time, and it had to be a modest affair so there was not that much planning. We were inviting all of the Whites, Johnny's parents, a few of the neighbors, the librarian, the pastor from our church, Mr. and Mrs. Kingsbury, and the owners of the cartridge factory where Johnny worked. Since it was in the spring we thought we might have the service outside, and if the weather held we could have a modest supper outside too. Otherwise we could use our parlor and dining room.

I sent Fitzy the guest list and was surprised when he sent a letter back saying he was coming to Coventry the next day. I hoped our plans were acceptable to him.

Fitzy and Florence arrived by coach, having taken the train from Springfield. The long trip by automobile, often requiring an overnight stay in Hartford, wasn't comfortable for Florence.

I dashed out to greet them. Fitzy looked old, and Florence, once she lifted the veil from her hat to hug me, looked wretched. Fear rose up in me.

"Something is wrong!" Were the first words I uttered. "What is wrong?" At that Florence leaned into Fitzy, who helped her into the kitchen. I made tea while Fitzy went to the tap room mumbling something about needing a stronger brew. I put saucers and cups and glasses on the table, all the while watching Florence and trying to make small talk, about how smoothly the inn was going, how well Edith was working out. Fitzy arrived with a bottle of brandy and poured each of us a small amount, even a glass for Edith.

"Millie, we have some very bad news." Fitzy was grave. Florence bent her head, put her hand up to her mouth and stifled a weak sob. My mind raced. He's lost his fortune was my first frantic thought.

Florence inhaled shakily and then sobbed out "Foster is gone." Fitzy, standing next to her, pulled her towards him and she put her arm around him. It was not what I was expecting, and I couldn't immediately comprehend it.

"What?"

"Foster is dead." Fitzy said. With his free hand he drank the brandy down in one gulp and snorted, almost choking.

"What happened?" I couldn't help but ask.

"A few days ago…" Florence started, "a few days ago a young man came to our door." She looked up at Fitzy, who sat down, poured himself another small glass and took her hand. "He asked if this was the Whites' residence and wanted to speak to Fitzy. When I invited him in he hesitated, but he followed me into the parlor."

Fitzy took over. "I couldn't imagine what he wanted. He looked like a vagabond, but spoke with a refined manner." He took another sip of brandy. "He didn't want to sit. He paced back and forth in front of the fireplace. I bade him sit several times but he waved me off. I knew something was very wrong. Finally he pulled out Foster's gold watch and handed it to me." Fitzy hesitated and took another sip. He cleared his throat. "I knew. I knew as soon as I saw the watch. I thought we did a good job of parenting, but maybe we were too permissive with him, maybe if we had been stricter.... I just thought he would outgrow his boyishness. I never imagined...." His voice trailed off.

Florence picked up where Fitzy left off. "The man's name was Samuel. He told us the whole story. He and Foster had become friends on the trek north. They helped each other through difficult times. When one of them needed money the other would help out. When one was sick the other cared for him. Samuel said they were almost inseparable until they finally made it to Skagway, where Foster met a girl and Samuel couldn't get him away for several months. Finally he was able to free Foster from the girl and they continued on. They staked a small claim, collected enough he said to pay some bills, but realized they weren't going to get rich. Then a strike in Nome reduced their town of Dawson City to a little outback. Foster decided to come home. Samuel tried to talk him out of it. Samuel told Foster he would travel part way with him but did not yet want go back to the States.

"Samuel told us of a real adventure they had. Foster had purchased a gun and was getting good at shooting. At one point they shot and ate a moose. They fancied themselves quite the adventurers. They met a number of interesting people, one a man called Bill Taft, who said he was going back to the States and make things right in Washington." Florence paused to sip the brandy. Fitzy took over.

"When they got back to Skagway Foster looked for the girl he had been with and found her with a ruffian. When a fight broke out the other man shot Foster. Shot him!" Fitzy's voice broke and Florence reached to touch his face. "Samuel said he lived for two days, but the doctor couldn't save him. The man ran away. The girl stayed by Foster's side until he passed. Samuel said Foster was lucid until the last few hours. He asked Samuel to send his things back home and Samuel said he would bring them. And then he was gone. They buried him in a cemetery in Skagway. He took all of Foster's money and had a stone engraved for him as he had asked: 'Here Lies Foster White, born in 1876, shot over a girl in 1899.'"

Edith, who hadn't even known Foster, was wiping her eyes with her towel. I was shocked into silence, still trying to take it all in, trying to understand that the little boy whose knee I had bandaged was gone.

Did I go wrong in not telling his parents that day when he fell off the penstock? Would punishment then have made him less of a daredevil? Or was he always in search of adventure that might bring him to a tragic end? My musings were interrupted.

"Her name was Lily. Samuel said Foster loved her and wanted to bring her back to live here." Florence sounded almost positive. "At least he found love." She looked up at Fitzy, who nodded.

"I am so sorry. I can hardly believe it. When did it happen?" I didn't know what else to say.

"In August." Florence spoke wistfully. "It was funny. I had a premonition one day in August. Foster's photograph fell off the mantel and the glass smashed. I don't think it was near the edge. It just fell off. Do you believe in signs, in the mystical?"

"Come now, Florence. You know there is no such thing as the mystical. That's just a sideshow gimmick." Fitzy was quick to discount it. But Florence was not so easily dissuaded.

"I don't know. I'm just not sure. Perhaps there is something there, a spirit, a soul...."

"Well, dear, if there is a spirit or soul, you can be sure that Foster's is in heaven. He was a good boy, a good man."

Fitzy sat down and put his head in his hands and now it was Florence's turn to comfort him.

I had to start cooking so I got up to get water boiling and stoke the stove.

"I hope you will be staying for supper and overnight too." I addressed them both. They stared blankly at each other, distracted by the main topic.

"Come now, you must stay. You must eat. You need to keep your strength up." I didn't add what I was uncharitably thinking: You do have other children and grandchildren.

Fitzy answered, "Yes, yes, we'll stay. You have room?" I nodded.

"Yes, your old room is still open." They looked at each other, but I couldn't tell what the look meant.

"Oh," Fitzy said, "I forgot. Samuel said Foster meant this to go to you." He dug into his coat, pulled out a book and handed it to me. I opened this foreign volume covered in ornate filigree, *The Way of the Bodhisattva,* and saw the inscription: "Millie – Karma will get you in the end. – Foster". For some strange reason this hit me harder than anything else had, and I too started to cry. I lifted my apron to stifle my sobs.

Fitzy moved to comfort me, making me sip some of the brandy. Edith began supper preparations and after a little while I helped. Florence also joined us. We were a family in pain but united in our menial daily chores.

Chapter 49

When Johnny got home the five of us ate in the kitchen and later Fitzy and Johnny settled into the taproom, where Fitzy told him the story. I had Edith run down and get the evening paper in case they wanted to sit and read it later. Florence helped in the kitchen as she once had, seeming to appreciate the distraction. After we had cleaned up we had tea at the table. I told Florence about the improvements and walked her around to see them. Everyone now seemed to accept Edith as part of the family.

I telephoned Fern that evening and asked her and Harold to join us on Friday for a couple of days, as it seemed that Fitzy and Florence might stay for a while. Then I called Fairy and tried to get her to come visit too, but she said she wasn't sure if she could.

I thought that being back here, in the place where the family was whole and perhaps had been happiest, may have been bittersweet for Fitzy and Florence, full of both good memories and also the emptiness those memories echoed. I couldn't tell them what was best for them to do. Only they knew if staying here would be a comfort. In the end they said they wanted to stay for a while, and I was happy they did. Florence had Fairy send down a trunk of clothes from Springfield.

Fern and Harold and their new daughter Susan arrived just in time for supper Friday evening. We were so busy I didn't even have time to comb my hair and pin it up properly so it was dropping into my face as I cooked and waited on everyone. Edith was the most help; if not for her the boarders wouldn't have been fed on time nor would our supper have been on the table for us when we all sat down. The table was not crowded although it was as full as it had been in my youth, and even though the mood was subdued, there was much talking and catching up.

Fern had already been told about Foster so there were no awkward questions at supper. Just to have a baby crawling around was enough to raise everyone's spirits.

The men retired to the taproom after the meal and once we'd cleaned up the women sat down for our evening tea as we always did. This was, I knew, when all the important talk transpired. Conversation turned to my impending marriage and everyone's offers of help, then to Edith's escape from the Blacks and how much she had become part of the family, then to Fairy and her son who was already walking, then to Fern and her family and home and plans for another child. When I asked about Freda, who was usually a strong presence at our family gatherings, Florence told us about her grand wedding and the prominent Springfield family she had married into. They had no children yet. Florence seemed to think Freda was reveling in the upper-crust society of her in-laws and had little time for her own family from Coventry.

Florence had little to say about herself except that she and Fitzy had been thinking of traveling to Alaska. This brought us to Foster, and gradually after some talk of his adventure we came around to tales of his life before he left, including his fall from the penstock. Florence was shocked to hear the details of that mishap. The only one unmentioned was Felicity. It seemed she was the very obvious empty chair, for we talked of everyone else, even poor dead Foster, but no one spoke her name.

As Edith and I finished up chores for the next day, Florence seemed tired and went to bed. The men came in for a few moments before Johnny went home and Fitzy joined Florence. Then Edith, who knew we'd be very busy in the morning, also went up. Fern, who had shooed Harold to bed, sat down across the table from me and opened the bottle of brandy the men had brought in from the taproom. She poured us each a little glass.

"So, do you love him?" Fern, so much like Edith, came right to the point.

"He's a good man, and I like him a lot. I know he will make a good husband and we will have a good life here."

"Felicity is at a school in Northampton. I hear she's doing well and getting good grades. She will be a college graduate when she finishes this summer."

The name pierced my heart like an arrow. No one had mentioned her the whole evening. Fern saw my reaction.

"So you still love her, don't you?" I nodded, then shook my head.

"I don't know. I'm trying not to think about her, but the memories slip in now and then. There's no sense in it, no future in it. I have to move on, and I have been, as best I could." Fern nodded. She understood. She was in love with Harold, and she knew that we can't choose whom to love.

"Well, good luck to you, Millie, whomever you choose. You have been a good and faithful sister, and I love you. We all do." She took my hands, raised me up from my chair and hugged me. "See you in the morning."

The next day was almost like old times as the women all cooked and set up for breakfast. It was even better than old times. Everyone knew what to do and no one avoided the tasks. Their joking made the work light. I wanted them to stay forever, but on Sunday evening Fern and Harold and Susan left for home. A week later Fitzy and Florence left. I wouldn't see any of them again until the week of the wedding.

Chapter 50

After the long winter and muddy spring May arrived like a princess, in gold and pink and gentle green finery.

Fern and Fairy came two weeks before the wedding to help me prepare. Not only did we have to clean the inn more thoroughly, we also had to plan for the food and flowers. Florence came a week after with a dress she had altered to fit me, a lovely cream-colored satin with lace and bows. I was so excited to have all the help that I couldn't express my gratitude. The inn fairly shone with polish. Johnny had painted doors and door jambs so they looked like new. The wedding would be in the church across the street, followed by a modest supper at the inn.

I wanted Fitzy and Florence to feel they were always welcome so I decided to leave the master bedroom set up for them. I fitted out Freda and Fairy's old room for Johnny and me. But for our wedding night Florence and Fern decorated the quiet room behind the parlor where we used to put newlyweds. That would be our honeymoon room.

As the days ticked off excitement at the inn grew. It was so much fun to have my family and their children with me.

Finally the day before the wedding arrived. I felt as though we were ready, but always some last minute preparation was forgotten and had to be tended to. Neighbors came with large bouquets of flowers to add to our already overflowing vases. Food that had been ordered had to be put in the root cellar and then prepared.

Fitzy, Orin and Harold took Johnny into the taproom after supper and some of the boarders joined them. The cigar smoke oozed out from under the door and traces drifted into the dining room. We could hear the laughter even in the kitchen, but we were having our own fun. Fitzy had kindly brought us a bottle of wine and a bottle of brandy. After supper we sat around the table and talked about the men. Shockingly Florence spoke of her first dates with Fitzy and how he tried to touch her breast. Then Fern told us about her first night with Harold. Mabel, Johnny's mother, shared some secrets of how her father, when Orin was courting her, had chased him down the street brandishing a shotgun. We laughed and joked until Fairy, not to be outdone, started to recount some of her adventures with boys from the neighborhood. At that point Florence declared it was time to shut the party down and sent us all to bed. The ladies waited for their gentlemen while I went to the room I still shared with Edith, who also didn't have any stories of her own.

My wedding day dawned sunny. It would be a beautiful day just as the almanac had predicted.

The women rushed around getting the food prepared and ready for our supper. I helped as much as I could but was so nervous that it wasn't much. I even broke a dish before I was sent back upstairs to dress.

The men were setting up tables on the lawn. As I looked down from my window it reminded me of our picnic so many years before, everyone bustling about, everyone excited.

Fern finally came up and helped me lace up my dress and then dressed herself. The ladies descended the front staircase, several in front of me and one behind to shield me from curious eyes. We crossed the road together. The men were already at the church, most seated except for Fitzy, who walked Florence down the aisle and then returned for me. I was frightened and excited. I barely remember my feet touching the ground. I could see Johnny at the altar waiting for me.

The service was not long and soon the minister was inviting everyone to join us across the street at the inn. Johnny kissed me and we walked out together. We were married. It was that simple. We were husband and wife.

The supper was set up quickly while we stood on the lawn shaking the hands of the well-wishers. Fitzy had even arranged for a photographer to come with a big box camera to photograph us and our parents. Fern and Fairy and Edith made magic happen with food and punch, and May wine appeared. Fitzy, who still had friends at the box factory, had invited several musicians, who were as good as any orchestra I ever heard. People danced. People ate. People drank, some until they could barely stand up. Still the band played on until it was dark and lanterns were set up. I was surprised to see the Chinese lanterns from years ago bouncing from the lines that held them.

I danced with Johnny, I danced with Fitzy, I danced with Orin, and I danced with Harold. Every time I slowed down to catch my breath someone would grab my hand and pull me out onto the carpet Fitzy had laid on the lawn. They plied me with food but mostly they plied me with wine until I was so dizzy I thought I would fall down. The day went so quickly I could barely remember it. I'd never had a day speed by so fast.

Finally I could see that the party was slowing down. Darkness had become dense and clean-up was starting. I was picking up glasses to bring into the house when Fitzy grabbed my elbow, called Johnny over and sent us both to our room behind the parlor.

"No cleaning for you tonight, young lady. It's time for you to retire."

The room was decked floor to ceiling with flowers, the rich smell almost overpowering. I barely found a spot to sit and take off my slippers.

Johnny took off his waistcoat and tie, pulled his suspenders down and removed his pants, shoes and socks. He stood in front of me in his shirt and shorts. He pulled me up and started to help me undress. He turned me around and unlaced my dress and pulled it gently off my shoulders. When only my petticoat was left he started to kiss my back, my shoulders, and my neck. He pressed against me and I could feel him hard on my lower back. Then he turned me around and kissed my mouth, holding me close. My mind flashed to Felicity pushing me up against the summer ice. Perhaps, I thought, this wouldn't be so bad.

It was over in minutes. I had expected more.

"I love you, Millie" was all he said before he rolled over and went to sleep.

Chapter 51

The next morning there was a knock at our door. When I answered it I found a tray on the floor. On it were breakfast and coffee, a rose and a bottle of champagne with a note: "Don't you dare come out before noon. – Fitzy"

The room had a back entrance into the first-floor bathroom. I knocked to make sure it was empty before I went in and washed up, still feeling lightheaded and out of my element.

When I returned Johnny was awake and drinking coffee. I had never expected him to be particularly romantic but he surprised me with kisses which progressed into more lovemaking that lasted longer than the previous night. I cannot say it was unpleasant, but I couldn't help but compare it to the gentle sensuous evenings I'd had with Felicity.

We lounged around the room until twelve as Fitzy had decreed, but when I heard the clock ring off the noon hour I got up and started to dress. Johnny watched me and in a disappointed voice said he thought we might stay a little later just this once.

"We have the rest of our lives," I said. "You won't be going home to your parents after work anymore. You'll be here with me. Isn't that enough?" He smiled and nodded. He actually had a very nice smile.

I carried several of the vases of flowers out into the dining room when I went to join the others to help with supper. Florence, Fern and Edith were doing the preparations and Fitzy was sitting at the table reading the paper. Harry was outside with Fairy watching the kids. Everyone looked up as I entered. I tried to be natural, going to the sink and helping Fern wash some of the vegetables.

"My, you're up early." Fitzy laughed at his own joke. They all glanced at me to see my reaction, but I kept washing as I turned it back at him. "Yes. Did you sleep all right or did we keep you up?"

He chuckled with the others, and to my relief they all went back to the business of making supper. Because of the wedding leftovers we didn't need to do much cooking.

Johnny came in before we sat down to eat. Conversation was about the wedding. Later Fitzy took Johnny aside to discuss plans for the inn and future finances, but Johnny wanted me to join them. He said I'd been running the inn almost totally on my own and I should know more about the business. This confused Fitzy, who said it should be the men who handled the business. But Johnny insisted I be included.

Summer was coming and we expected business to pick up. It had already started to. How would we handle it? We were able to put his mind at ease. Fairy had said she was thinking about moving back down and could help us so we would have plenty of staff here. Fitzy, though reluctant to have his last daughter and his grandson leave Springfield, saw the merit in the plan and said he and Florence would visit often. Later he took me aside and told me to be sure she didn't get into any more trouble.

Freda, Florence reminded me, had married well in Springfield and did not even want to acknowledge that she came from Coventry, so we might never see her again. I tried not to let it my relief show.

After a week they all left, Fairy to pack and ship her things. Fern joined Harold in Mansfield but said she'd be back often.

Only Johnny, Edith and I were left to keep the inn going, and we were busy at it.

We had contracted for a farmer who had an extra wagon to bring visitors from the train station. The wagon was to be clean and his son would drive it. So the farmer would earn some extra cash while guests reaped the benefit of a larger group at a lower cost than the regular coach.

The mood was always festive when visitors arrived, and the wagon added to the sense of adventure. The more well-to-do waited for the coach to provide them a more comfortable and dignified ride.

Most visitors were millworkers from Willimantic looking for a vacation from the noise and dirt of the city. With so many coal-fired factories there the smell and dust of the coal smoke hung in the air. We put most of these people on the third floor, filling the back first, wherever we didn't have boarders. Although their rooms were not the most elegant they found it a great improvement over their tenements, and they were treated to hearty meals, fresh air and a beautiful lake where they could picnic or hire a boat or boat ride.

Word had gotten around and we were getting enough reservations to almost fill the inn on Saturdays and Sundays and stay reasonably full the rest of the week.

Strangely, Johnny made a major purchase without consulting me or Fitzy. He ordered a coin-operated player piano. When it came he described it as something that would make us rich because people would always want to pay to hear it. It was an expense I could not understand. We put it in the parlor and people did indeed enjoy it, but I told him that once the fancy wore off we might consider selling it.

Thankfully Fairy arrived later in May just as the summer season came upon us. On rainy days we organized checkers competitions and charades and little plays the children could put on. For the men we offered poker games Wednesday and Friday evenings in the taproom, attracting enough of a crowd that our beer flowed so freely it never got stale. For the women we offered trips to some of the mill showrooms, where they could purchase fabric made in the mill at reduced rates. We occasionally had dances and hosted weddings. Our first summer season was as fine as I could ever remember.

Then I found I was pregnant.

Johnny had been at first a thoughtful love-maker. I was his new wife and he was considerate of me. As the busy months rolled by and we were often bone-tired at the end of our day his lovemaking became what seemed like a requirement he had to fulfill. Since he was the barkeep he usually had a few beers in the taproom with the patrons.

Sometimes it would be more than a few and he would come to bed and roughly mount me as though I were merely a convenience. Sometimes he just flopped down and fell asleep, or was in bed and asleep before I even got to our room. At those times I was grateful he was just too tired. I never criticized him—I wouldn't think of it—but sometimes Fern and I did talk about how our husbands were "in the sack." Harold and Fern were still in love and though their lovemaking was not as frequent as it once had been, she said he was someone whom she enjoyed and who enjoyed her also. I chalked up our less-than-perfect bed time to tiredness and overwork. But gradually I came to wish he would just leave me alone. On rare occasions he was more of his earlier self, gentle and thoughtful. Sometimes his kisses were little pecks, but often I felt I was being engulfed, and when drunk he slobbered.

Then when I became pregnant and thought I had an excuse to avoid some of the intimacies, he pressed me.

That first month I was late and realized I might be pregnant I started to notice subtle changes. My body felt fuller, richer. My breasts became enlarged and tender. I started to feel tired. I was almost never tired and almost never sick so I noted this distinct change in my health. I had strange cravings, some for food I rarely had eaten.

I told Johnny. He seemed pleased, and was soon telling everyone the news. I was almost embarrassed by his frequent repetitions of his new status as father-to-be. My family was happy at the prospect of another new addition, especially Fitzy and Florence.

From what I could tell, I would probably give birth the following spring, maybe in April.

I was going to be a mother.

Chapter 52

The autumn saw fewer guests. Even so I was very grateful to have Fairy and Edith to pick up much of the workload I now seemed too tired to carry. I still did more than my share but left the heavier tasks to them.

Several of the boys had become so helpful we decided to reduce their room rate. Because of their labors in the garden we called them the farmers "Mac" and "Donald." Thanks to their skills the fall harvest was the largest we'd ever had and we'd be able to put up bushels of potatoes and turnips and can much of the surplus. We were rich with food. The scale that Edith and I named Ethel now held a prominent place at the top of one of our cabinets and was used to weigh our produce before water-bath processing. Ethel was never brought down without giggles from Edith and me.

Late one afternoon while we were canning string beans Mac came in and sat down at table where we were working. He was a tall and gangly fellow with shocking red hair which never seemed to sit flat, springing out in all directions. Mac's disposition was the opposite of Donald's. Whereas Donald seemed morose, Mac was always cheerful and silly. Mac watched us for a while, realized what our next steps would be, and jumped in to lend a hand carrying the heavy kettle from the stove to the table so we could extract the canned jars and cool them on the racks.

I knew Mac's last name was McGill, but I don't think I'd ever heard his Christian name until that day.

"Eddie, could you fill this pot for me?" Fairy had her hands full. We were trying to get all the canning done before we had to set up for the next day.

Mac jumped up and took the large pot from Fairy, carrying it to the sink. I happened to notice him pause almost imperceptibly and look down with appraising eyes at the full figure of Fairy, who was half his height. For the rest of the evening I watched their interactions. Mac didn't go leave until we had finished, even staying to have the cup of tea we offered him. Donald had gone up long before, complaining of a sore back. I had the impression that Mac had persuaded Donald to work with him in the garden. I watched nonchalantly as Fairy and Mac talked and laughed together, and thought to myself it was time for Fairy to get along with her life.

Day by day the little flirtations escalated ever so slightly. By Saturday, Mac was pushing Fairy's son Daniel on the swing while Fairy watched from a lawn chair, bundled against the autumn chill. Daniel laughed as each push seemed to send him higher and higher. Fairy laughed. Mac laughed. A bond was obviously growing.

I wrote to Fitzy and Florence that one of our nicest boy boarders was favoring Fairy. I described him and said I hoped they wouldn't think this mill boy was beneath her. I told them he worked at Kingsbury's and was actually two years younger than Fairy although that didn't seem to be a barrier.

Several days later I received a letter back from Fitzy. He wrote he had talked to a manager at Kingsbury's and not only did they think highly of Mac, they were giving him a promotion. He said he and Flo would be down to visit next week and they would not let on that they knew of the attraction. I wrote back asking them to stay for Thanksgiving and I also sent an invitation to Fern and Harold, thinking it would be fun to have a big holiday together.

I was beginning to get a stomach. I donned one of Freda's old dresses, which was too big but afforded my expanding abdomen ample room. I was able to cinch up its looseness with the long apron strings, pulling the bunched gathers over the waist so it wouldn't be too long. Edith offered to hem it shorter, and I was reminded of Felicity bowed over her sewing. I became unexpectedly melancholy and had to run to the bathroom to compose myself. I found that carrying this child brought on emotions I usually paid no attention to.

Fitzy and Flo arrived the Sunday before Thanksgiving, intending to stay a week. We had several turkeys picked out for the supper and Mac was fattening them apart from the others. It was getting so I didn't know what I would do without Mac. Johnny was a hard worker and good contributor, but Mac seemed the more attentive. When Johnny was working in the taproom Mac would be helping in the kitchen or in the barn or with the chickens.

We had become so accustomed to the abundance provided by growing our own food that we were considering going a step further and raising a litter of pigs to add to our modest inn farm. With Mac and Donald to help we could do it, although we might have to pen them up the hill where they would not be so close to the village. After I discussed it with Johnny and Mac, who volunteered to help, we talked to the farmer close by. He said he had a sow he would sell us in the spring and we could board her there if we cleaned up and fed her and the piglets ourselves. We thought this was a fine idea.

The kitchen table was almost full the first supper after Fitzy and Florence's arrival. Along with them were Fairy, Edith, Johnny and I and of course little Daniel, and then I had decided to invite Mac to dine with us rather than with the other boarders. This I knew was an unspoken acknowledgement of the friendship that had developed between him and Fairy. In his acceptance he seemed shy but grateful. Fairy was surprised and even shy about it herself. Fitzy was of course the good-natured but polite head of the family, making small talk and chattering about Springfield, then asking Mac about the local mills and news from the factories. Mac though bashful was up to the challenge, sharing new innovations at the box factory and other news he'd picked up from his friends.

Afterward the fellows retired to the taproom as was their usual custom while the women cleaned up. We were glad to have the men gone so we could talk about the main subject tonight, Mac.

"So, Mac seems nice, and smart. What is he doing? I heard he was helping out here?" Florence said this to no one in particular as she carried dishes and piled them up in the sink.

"Yes, he has been so helpful. You have no idea how much we have come to depend upon him." I answered, not wanting Fairy to feel she had to.

"Donald has been pitching in too, but I think Mac is especially helpful." Now Edith was adding her opinion.

I could see Fairy's eyes move back and forth between us as we discussed this man who had become her friend. I think she wanted to speak, but each time someone else spoke before she could.

I didn't think things had progressed any further than flirtation, and hardly even that, but it was now obvious to Fairy that Mac was being accepted by the family. Why, he was even in the taproom with the menfolk. Perhaps she even felt a little nervous about it. Perhaps she wasn't sure of her feelings about him but felt she was almost being pushed towards him.

Our questions were soon answered when Fairy finally spoke. "He's a nice boy." She hesitated and looked around at us as we all paused in our work to hear what she was going to say. "He's a nice boy, and I like him, but I don't see what all the fuss is about. We're not courting or anything." We held her gaze. She colored. All I could think was that Mac had a challenge ahead. We went back to work talking of everything but Mac.

Chapter 53

As my pregnancy progressed Johnny, although as attentive as usual, spent more time in the taproom with his customers. I couldn't fault him. I was not the thin energetic girl he had married. We were rarely intimate and when we were it was when he'd had a few too many beers and wanted me to pleasure him.

Mac was often in the kitchen now helping Fairy, drying dishes, putting them away, and even serving when we needed an extra hand. With them and Edith the kitchen was the liveliest room in the house, and sometimes Johnny would stay back and help or sit at the table and read his paper. He no longer seemed to carry any animosity towards Edith and would even joke with her over a boarder or tease her about saving a special morsel for Donald. She took it all in good stride and could give it back when she'd had enough.

Edith worked hard and over time she gained the respect of everyone in the family. She seemed happier than I'd ever seen her. Fairly glowing with self-confidence and good health. With decent meals and without the worry of living on the edge she had blossomed into a very pretty lass indeed, and her glasses served only to make her look more clever. The dark hair characteristic of her family was clean and shining like ebony and she'd filled out, no longer the cadaverous scarecrow who showed up at our door. Only once did I see her with the fearful look she had habitually worn when in the company of her family. That was when a wagon drove by with banging and clanking that must have reminded her of the travels with the Blacks. Rarely did a cloud now cover her countenance. While not as jolly as Fairy she enjoyed a good joke and laughed along with the rest of us, even occasionally at herself. She'd become my confidant and knew many of the family secrets, which she was cautious about sharing. The only thing I never told her was of my nights with Felicity.

The weeks of my pregnancy seemed to drag on, each more difficult than the previous one. Back pain punctuated my movements. My sleep, now always on my side, was uncomfortable and little kicks sometimes woke me. Spring was near. Rains had superseded snow. As the ground thawed, mud became an unwelcome addition to our cleaning routines. Johnny put boards down on the walkways to minimize it as much as possible. Mac and Donald had saved some seeds from last year and were preparing to plant peas and onions as soon as they could work the soil. Once planting began in mid-March, Fairy sent Daniel out to play in the garden and "help" the boys. He would come in with dirt up to his ears but happy as only a child can be. Mac was good with Daniel, and Fairy and all of us noticed. One evening when Fairy had gone to bathe Daniel and put him to bed I took Mac into the pantry.

"Mac, how serious are you about Fairy?" I must have been more anxious about the question than he was since he seemed content just to wipe dishes next to her.

"What?" My directness must have surprised him.

"You know, Fairy. Are you courting her or waiting for her to make the first move?" He looked blankly at me, taking a couple seconds before he realized what I was asking. Then he blushed.

"I don't know what to do," was his honest reply.

"This is what you do. Ask her to help you in the root cellar. You know we have a lot of spring cleaning to do in there now that the fresh ice is up. When she goes in with you give her a kiss. You know how to kiss, don't you?"

His eyebrows went up so far they almost met his ragged front forelock. He looked at me as though I were a foreign object. I grabbed the front of his shirt, pulled his face down to mine and kissed him very nicely on the lips.

He pulled back and fell into the flour bin, sending the flour scuttle flying and puffs of white everywhere.

"There. That's how you do it."

I turned around and went to the door. "And don't you say a word of this to anyone!" I closed it after me.

I'm not sure what possessed me. Perhaps it was the moods I found washing over me like waves. Perhaps it was my impatience, or perhaps I just liked him and wanted them to find their way to each other. Whatever it was it must have worked. He never mentioned it, but several days later I noticed a marked change in their interactions. She was no longer treating him like a brother, and he was hovering more than ever. I watched as she slowly handed him a plate to dry and when he took it his fingers touched hers and lingered for a second and their eyes met. It was the romantic stage I had been waiting for, and I prided myself at being a possible accelerant to the slow burn.

While this romance was igniting I also noticed that another was quietly developing, possibly without even the participants' knowledge. It was Edith and Johnny. While I would have appreciated some love-making, Johnny did not seem willing to provide it. I didn't ask, although some evenings I would kiss him in a way that might have aroused him. He would only kiss me back and make no attempt to touch me. But I could see little signs between the two of them that told me a closeness was growing. Johnny sometimes helped with the dishes. He began coming to the kitchen earlier and lent a hand chopping vegetables. During these times when we were all there together the mood was usually light and we frequently horsed around with each other. A towel might be snapped at someone, a joke made at another's expense, a spoonful of water splashed into a face or a sliver of ice slipped down a back. All of it was silly and fun and made our chores seem much lighter. I didn't think either of them realized what was happening nor did I think they would ever do something to hurt me, but strange things had been set in motion that I thought might make for discomfort later.

But I never would have guessed what the future held.

Chapter 54

I was close to term. The midwife had visited once and said she would come when we sent for her. She had a telephone so we could contact her quickly and she could arrive in minutes.

My moodiness seemed to accelerate the closer I came to giving birth. I was full of fear, afraid our child might die, afraid I might die, afraid we wouldn't be able to care for it properly.

I was melancholy, watching Johnny and Edith and thinking of my lost love. I found the letter Felicity had left for me and cried over it, blurring the ink. Then I tore it up and stuffed it into an old shoe.

I began to get restless and wanted to be outside helping to plant the garden.

Then a letter came from Fern. Felicity had graduated from her school the previous summer and moved to New York City. She had taken up residence with some women who owned a hotel, working for them as a manager and consultant. She had, Fern wrote, become a designer for their interior décor, and was doing quite well. Fern went on about other family news, but this news of Felicity was unnerving. I went into labor.

Edith called the midwife. I was not ready but all the preparations had been made and I was taken to the upstairs front room where Felicity was born. Abundant spring flowers were brought in to cheer me and the room must have looked as Florence described it when she was there almost twenty-three years before. Daffodils, narcissus and tulips overflowed their vases, but I had only moments to notice before the pain came again.

How is it we all come into the world in the same way but none of us can recall it? Something so momentous should be a thing seared into our memory, never to be forgotten, but I suppose as infants our brains are not equipped to grasp it.

My daughter came the way I must have, wailing and writhing and ready for life. Once she quieted down and was placed on my breast the world seemed like the most beautiful place I could ever have imagined.

Johnny came in, held the baby, took my hand and kissed me. If he was disappointed he did not have a son he didn't say anything. He had hopes for more children, lots of them, and this was only the first.

Tired and drained, I slept until I felt Jenny move and then I fed her and slept some more.

Jenny was the name I had chosen, Florence's mother's name, and although I'd never met her, I thought she must have been very special.

I was in love again. I didn't care if Johnny and Edith had a flirtation. I didn't care if Felicity was in New York City. I had Jenny.

Florence and Fitzy arrived the next day with toys and baby clothes. Johnny was an attentive father, wanting to hold her and hold me, and he forgot Edith for a while. The third day Fern came with her daughter Susan to stay for several days. I was being pampered until I could no longer lie in bed another hour, so I took little Jenny, all pink and bundled, and joined the family in the kitchen where supper was being prepared.

Johnny took a small carriage from storage and set Jenny up it. "Well, I think we should teach her kitchen duties at a young age." He laughed over his joke along with along with Fitzy, who in an unusual turn was helping prepare supper.

"Millie, see what they have me doing in your absence? They are merciless taskmasters." He tipped his head towards the three women at the table. "You needn't be here. We have it fully under control."

"I couldn't spend another moment in that bed." But I sat down, feeling a little light-headed. Fern poured me a cup of tea and pushed a plate with a couple crackers on it in front of me. I drank and nibbled and felt oddly on the periphery. I, usually at the center of a pinwheel of busyness, was now relegated to the edge. I felt out of place.

I watched everyone at their tasks. Fairy seemed to work steadily but not as quickly as the others. Fern, Edith and Florence teamed up like a machine, one washing the potatoes and passing them to the other, who cut them up and handed them on to the third, who put them into the pot with water and onions she had sliced. Edith was fitting into the family as though born to it. The only difference was her dark hair, almost the opposite coloring of Fern's and Florence's. Her skin though was pale and in contrast to her hair seemed almost white. My family had more color to their cheeks and lips. Edith was tall like Fern, and both had an economy of movement that made their actions smooth and clean, no useless swinging of their arms, no extra steps. I had never before been an observer watching them work together. It was a pleasure to see them move almost as one. Usually I was too much a part of the process to see its beauty.

Fitzy was fussing and clanging about as though he were doing a big job, but he seemed to be mostly talking and shuffling loose vegetables around. Kitchen work, as he explained, was not his usual job. Florence laughed and asked what his usual job was. This was enough to send him to the taproom with a falsely exaggerated huff.

Johnny, wisely staying clear of the women, was now busily setting up the boarders' tables for supper.

When all the food was on the stove the women took a moment to sit with me. Edith picked up Jenny, who had been sleeping, and cradled her as she brought her to me to nurse.

"That baby is so quiet I worry about her." Florence sounded a little concerned. "Freda was always crying. She never seemed to stop. Fairy, you were not as fussy as Freda, but Fern, you were just like Jenny; you never cried either. Millie, you and Felicity were quiet too. You seemed to comfort each other."

Everyone turned to Florence. Neither Florence nor Fitzy had ever mentioned Felicity to me since they moved away. Florence looked around and suddenly realized she had approached a taboo topic. She changed the subject. "Well, she certainly seems to feed well." I nodded.

"Yes, she does."

"I was such a fussy mother with Freda," Florence reminisced, "but I couldn't be with the rest of you. By the time you came along, Fairy, I wasn't worried about those little things that seemed to concern me at first."

Supper was soon on the table. We served the boarders, ate our own meal, and started the cleanup. Johnny had gotten into the habit of picking up the dishes from the boarders' tables first, then collecting ours, and as Edith washed, he dried. They had replaced the team of Fairy and Mac, who in their courting had broken several dishes and were now relegated to other tasks. They gathered the linens, shaking them out in the fresh air and putting them in the laundry, then swept the dining room and, as best they could, the kitchen. Armed with brooms, they occasionally took little swats at each other but finally did get the job done. I thought it was fun to see that young love blossom. Then I realized I was not that old. I watched Edith and Johnny. If there was still a flirtation they were keeping it hidden.

Johnny approached me that evening. He had not done so in months. He kissed me and rolled onto me but I told him it wasn't time yet, and he had me hold him as he moved against my hand. When he finished and rolled over I asked him, "Edith is nice, isn't she? She's fit into our household just as I'd hoped." Johnny grunted and was silent for a minute. Then I heard him snore.

Chapter 55

The next day when I woke Johnny was already up. I rose, washed up and started to feed Jenny. I sat in the rocker, looking out the window onto a spring day. The birds were singing; my child was at my breast. A wonderful sense of wellbeing washed over me. Then a crow landed in the tree and frightened the birds away, and suddenly the feeling of wellbeing became a wave of fear and dread, an omen of change, I thought. Something was going to happen. Jenny must have felt me stiffen for she stopped suckling, looked at me and began to cry. I soothed her and soon she was suckling again.

When I went down to breakfast I found Fitzy, Florence and Fern had packed and left their suitcases by the door.

"Leaving already?" I asked, knowing I sounded disappointed.

"Yes, we've got some things to do at home." Florence also seemed disappointed. We all sat down to breakfast and then they left with promises to visit again soon.

Starting to feel more like my old self, I helped with the cleanup and after that tackled some of my easier chores, not lifting heavy loads or attempting the more demanding cleaning. Every now and then I would poke my head into Jenny's carriage and watch her sleep, her peaceful face like an angel's.

As the weeks went by I found myself feeling much as I did prior to my pregnancy, strong, full of energy, healthy, hearty and happy. Jenny was growing and becoming more animated. When I looked into the carriage she seemed to recognize me and would swing her arms about and giggle.

I had returned to my former self, but my marriage to Johnny became more difficult. He often spent whole evenings in the taproom, from which loud laughs and shouts sometimes emerged. When he did visit the kitchen he'd choose to help not me but more likely Edith, and sometimes Fairy.

Fairy and Mac were now courting openly and everyone thought well of the pair. Mac told me he was waiting to propose until his mother gave him a ring she'd promised so he could do it properly. We were having Mac's parents over to supper, and I thought that would be enough to calm any fears they might have about Fairy and their son.

Johnny had regressed into careless lovemaking when we did have the time to consummate our marriage vows. I felt he wanted only to have more children so as to lessen his burden at the inn. It might take a few years to get the family to the size he wanted. We rarely talked.

Fitzy could see the gap between us and I think he thought it was because I was avoiding my duties as a wife. He asked me why Johnny seemed so unhappy, but I had no good answer for him.

Then in the fall it happened. The idea that had hung over me for months, the sense of foreshadowing the crow had brought, was looming close. Something was coming to fruition.

A perfect autumn day dawned and I was going about my regular chores putting breakfast on the table for the boarders and ourselves. Fairy was washing canning jars to put up our garden's abundant crops when Mac came home later. I fed Jenny, who was not only nursing but starting to eat small crushed-up bits of our food. Edith, the hardest worker at the inn, was changing bedclothes and preparing to do laundry. I went to the market to pick up some spices, salt and sugar for the canning. When I got back Edith came into the kitchen with a basket of sheets and pillow slips, looking troubled. After she emptied the basket into the laundry she came over to me.

"There's something strange upstairs. Can you come up and see?" I followed her up and she pointed me into the bedroom Johnny and I shared. "Over there, on the pillow." She stood at the door while I went in.

I knew what it was as soon as I saw it, even from across the room, and I motioned Edith away. There, on my pillow on top of a small envelope, was a thimble. My heart pounded. I caught my breath and my mouth went dry. I picked up the thimble, inspecting it. It was much more worn than when I'd given it to Felicity, polished shiny from use. She had kept it all this time. I picked up the envelope and smelled it, sat down and carefully opened it.

My Dearest Millie,

I have thought of you almost every day since we parted. Fern has kept me apprised of your circumstances. I was crushed when you were married, but happy to hear you have a child.

After years of schooling, I have moved to New York City and have a position as a designer. This has given me the independence that I need.

I do not want to burden you so I will only ask you once. If you are happy in Coventry you should stay, but I want you in N.Y. with me. So if you are not happy, please, please come to New York with me.

I will wait for you tomorrow afternoon, 4 p.m. at the Coventry station.

With All My Love,
Felicity

I was stunned. I re-read the letter several times, smelled it again, then held it to my breast. It was shocking to think that Felicity had made her way into my home and placed this letter on my pillow.

She had been here.

Where was she now? I wanted so much to see her. Four years had passed. Was she still the same Felicity I remembered? How could I take such a chance without knowing?

My mind was in turmoil, my heart still racing. I couldn't think. I had to get out, to walk, to try to sort this out. I went downstairs and told Edith I needed to go back to the store for something I'd forgotten. I threw on my shawl and crossed the street to the sidewalk. This was better. When I was moving I could think more clearly. I walked up to the lake and back, then made the round trip again, not caring what would go through Edith's mind when I didn't come right back. I had to think. What would I do? Yes, I could stay with Johnny, but my future here was predictable, and Johnny might not even be true after a while. What a decision! Finally I decided I would pack, take Jenny and go to the station. I would know, I thought, as soon as I saw Felicity. I could make the decision then, right there and then. I could go or I could stay.

I was uncomfortable the whole evening, chafing at my dilemma. I couldn't sit still. I was in constant motion. The dishes got done more quickly than ever. Edith must have sensed something, even perhaps connected it to the thimble on the pillow, but she didn't say anything. Johnny went to the taproom and when he came upstairs was distant as usual; he just fell into bed and rolled towards the wall. I went through my few sets of clothing and folded them carefully, readying them to pack into my satchel. I put Jenny's little nightgowns and nappies in a pile near mine.

I couldn't sleep. I lay there and listened to Johnny's breathing, slow and deep. I thought about how my leaving would affect him. Would he be devastated? Would he be upset for a while, but find a new mate in Edith? Was I being insane to even consider leaving? My life wasn't that bad here; it was actually pretty good. What was I thinking? What would my parents think? Could I ever come back if it didn't work out? And yet, I couldn't help myself. I could only think of that first kiss in the root cellar, those nights of gentle passion. I must have slept some but I wasn't sure.

The next morning dawned. I made breakfast early, had a little more coffee than usual and kissed Johnny as he went off to work, thinking I might never do that again. Then, trying to be nonchalant, I worked through the morning chores more quickly than usual. I called on a local man to pick me up at three o'clock and drive me to the train station, telling him I was meeting a friend there. I told Edith the same. If I decided to leave I didn't know how I'd tell Johnny. I didn't want to leave a letter that might be found before I came back, if I decided to come back. If I decided to leave I thought I might mail a letter from the station or leave a note there to be sent back. I packed paper and envelopes, one addressed to Fern, who, if I did leave, would be the one who might smooth things over with the family. So very complicated was this possible running away turning out to be. How silly to think I could or would escape–and why? My life was not that bad.

Finally, after packing and trying to be discreet with the bag, I met the wagon in front of the inn, Jenny on my hip.

It was an odd trip to the station, one I rarely made, and I thought about that as I looked back at the little village of my youth. The thimble and cartridges clinked in my pocket.

The station came into view. I was excited and frightened all at once. Would she be there? Jenny and I got down from the wagon and the man handed my bag down to me. I hesitated a second before entering the small lobby. She wasn't there. The station master looked at me and pointed towards the platform. I went out onto it and the sight of her took my breath away. She was more beautiful than ever, a woman now, no longer the thin sickly child I remembered. She walked over to me, kissed Jenny, took my hand and kissed it, then kissed me gently on the lips.

"I missed you" was all she said.

Historic Convergences and Divergences

In an attempt to bring a slice of Coventry's history to life I tried to include businesses and buildings as they were in the time period this novel covers, early 1870 to 1899. Convergences and divergences from the historical timeline are outlined below. The column on the left lists the date in the novel.

1880 – The Bidwell House was built in 1822 and run as an inn by the Bidwell family until 1881. The building also served as the post office and had a ballroom. In the early 1900s a second-floor porch was added, and around the same time it became a trolley stop.

1880 – The Kingsbury Box Factory made paper boxes and labels from 1864 to 1915. Coventry was one of several company sites.

1880 – The Mason Cartridge Factory (later the Phoenix Metallic Cartridge Company and then the American Metallic Cartridge Company) manufactured ammunition 1866 to 1903.

1880 – Wellwood's General Store, built in 1787, is the oldest standing general store building in the nation.

1886 – Jack the Ripper's murders in London's Whitechapel district, 1888

1887 – H.W. Kimbal Satinet Factory fire in Coventry, 1884

1888 – *The Adventures of Huckleberry Finn* published 1885

1889 – Ford Model T built 1888-1889 (by 1903-04 several Coventry businessmen owed autos, one a Stanley Steamer).

1889 – First assembly line 1913

1889 – Coca-Cola first sold 1886

1890 – Women's Christian Temperance Union founded 1880

1891 – Ragtime popular from 1895 to 1918

1892 – Blizzard of 1888

1893 – Philadelphia and Reading Railroad trouble in 1893 caused a run on the banks.

1894 – Klondike Gold Rush 1896-1899

1895 – Financial panic of 1893 caused a run on the banks; 500 closed, along with 15,000 businesses. Stocks fell, unemployment skyrocketed, and soup kitchens opened to feed the destitute.

1897 – *Dracula* published 1897

1899 – Charlotte Perkins Gilman, originally from Connecticut, published *The Yellow Wallpaper* 1892

1899 – William Howard Taft was a resident of Skagway during the Gold Rush, 1899

1899 – South Coventry Water Supply, 1870s-1899

1899 – Wurlitzer's first coin-operated player piano, 1898

Shetucket River Milltown Series

Other novels by Diana K. Perkins set in Eastern Connecticut

Singing Her Alive, set in Willimantic, Connecticut, is the compelling story of two mill girls, presented to the reader as a fictional memoir set in two timelines. The primary story, in the late1800s, unfolds when the present-day granddaughter of one of the mill girls discovers a secret journal, thrusting her into a journey towards identity and place. *Singing Her Alive* has won numerous awards and garnered five-star reviews on Amazon and other sites.

Jenny's Way, based on a local legend, is a fictional tale set in Baltic, Connecticut. The story spans the four decades from 1930 through the 1960s. It follows the entwined lives of three families, each with their own destiny, weaving together their dark and light threads throughout the years. These families create a tapestry of local color: a good, hardworking farm family, a troubled mill-working family and an extended family of women who are supported by the kindnesses of the mill boys they serve service.

Diana's Pool is based on a legend local to Eastern Connecticut. Set in the small town of Chaplin, it explores the story about a favorite swimming hole on the Natchaug River.

Did a girl named Diana jump into the pool and never come out alive? Was it an accident? Was it deliberate? Was it murder?

http://dianakperkins.com